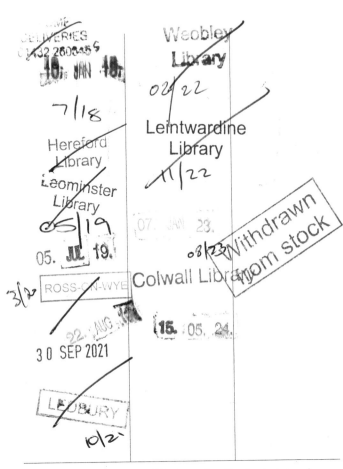
Please return/renew this item by the last date shown

**Herefordshire
Libraries**

*Herefordshire
Council*

Royal Spring Babies

*Unexpected royal heirs
for two Italian princes!*

Dante and Enzo Affini,
Venice's hottest doctors, have a secret…
they're also Italian princes! Now, to save
their inheritance and the family name,
they'll need to marry and produce heirs—*stat*!

For Nurses Shay Labadie
and Aubrey Henderson a six-month stint
in Italy teaching new nurses is the escape
they both need. But as romance blooms in
the spring sunshine they find themselves
with new roles entirely…as royal mums!

Read Dante's story in
His Pregnant Royal Bride
by Amy Ruttan

Read Enzo's story in
Baby Surprise for the Doctor Prince
by Robin Gianna

Available now!

Dear Reader,

Deciding to set this book in Venice, Italy, was easy—such a magical place! Then my editor Laura asked if I'd like to have the book be part of a duet with the wonderful Amy Ruttan. Brainstorming the story with Amy was a lot of fun—as was figuring out the last details with Amy and Laura poolside in San Diego at the RWA conference. A writer's life is rough! ;-)

In the story Aubrey thinks she's going to Italy to nurse there, and to support her pregnant friend Shay… Until Aubrey meets a gorgeous Italian man, Enzo Affini, and can't resist a hot one-night fling. Except when she returns to Venice two months later she learns he's the doctor she has to work for!

Enzo is suspicious of Shay showing up in his brother's life, and when Aubrey comes to work for him he wonders about her, too! Until a shocking event forces him to rethink his life and what's most important to him.

This story is about trust and betrayal and learning that the things we may believe about ourselves aren't always true. I hope you enjoy it!

Robin xoxo

BABY SURPRISE FOR THE DOCTOR PRINCE

BY
ROBIN GIANNA

First published in Great Britain 2017
By Mills & Boon, an imprint of HarperCollins*Publishers*
1 London Bridge Street, London, SE1 9GF

Large Print edition 2017

© 2017 Robin Gianakopoulos

ISBN: 978-0-263-06722-4

Printed and bound in Great Britain
by CPI Antony Rowe, Chippenham, Wiltshire

After completing a degree in journalism, then working in advertising and mothering her kids, **Robin Gianna** had what she calls her 'awakening'. She decided she wanted to write the romance novels she'd loved since her teens, and now enjoys pushing her characters towards their own happily-ever-afters. When she's not writing, Robin's life is filled with a happily messy kitchen, a needy garden, a wonderful husband, three great kids, a drooling bulldog and one grouchy Siamese cat.

Books by Robin Gianna

Mills & Boon Medical Romance

The Hollywood Hills Clinic

The Prince and the Midwife

Midwives On-Call at Christmas

Her Christmas Baby Bump

Flirting with Dr Off-Limits
It Happened in Paris…
Her Greek Doctor's Proposal
Reunited with His Runaway Bride

Visit the Author Profile page at millsandboon.co.uk for more titles.

I'd like to thank my duet partner, Amy Ruttan, for being so great to work with.
Let's do it again sometime, Amy!

Also, another huge shout-out to my wonderful friend Meta Carroll for helping me with the medical scenes in the story—thanks and smooches!

**Praise for
Robin Gianna**

'Robin Gianna writes stories that will draw you in with their sensuality and emotion and this one was a beauty… I loved this story from start to finish.'

—*Goodreads* on
The Prince and the Midwife

CHAPTER ONE

AUBREY HENDERSON LIFTED her face to the lagoon breeze and smiled, soaking in the incredible history, vivid colors, and sheer amazement that was Venice, Italy. How lucky was she to have snagged a temporary job here? She might have spent only two days in Venice before leaving for her two-month nursing job in Rome, but every detail of those hours felt etched in her brain.

Which included every detail of her illicit, probably ill-advised, and beyond wonderful fling with Enzo Affini. That one night felt burned into her mind—and body, as well—and just the thought of him made her silly heart both skip a beat and burn with annoyance.

Maybe they'd left it a little vague, but hadn't he implied he'd be in touch? What exactly they'd said to one another when they'd parted in the wee hours of the morning didn't seem too clear anymore, but still. She'd expected he'd at least call her while she was in Rome, since he knew she was coming back to Venice around now.

Knowing she might run into him in the flesh had her feeling nervous and excited and ticked off all over again for making her wonder if she'd ever hear from him. Then ticked off at herself for wondering at all.

Then annoyed even more when she realized that when the phrase *in the flesh* had come to mind, an instant all-too-sexy vision of the man's glorious body made her feel a little breathless.

Ridiculous. Time to concentrate on why she'd come to Venice, which had nothing to do with a handsome Italian prince who was obviously the love-'em-and-leave-'em type. Which was okay. She didn't care if she saw him or not. In fact, she had no desire at all to see the guy, since he clearly didn't want to see her.

No, she'd come here before to support her friend Shay, who'd recently married Enzo's brother, Dante. Now she was here to work in the clinic, enjoy that adventure, and meet with the art and architecture preservation society she'd donated more money to in her mother's memory.

Her mom had always been fascinated with Venice and its incredible history, and it had only been her fear of travel and crowds that had kept her from coming to explore it. Seeing the fresco she and her mom had "adopted," paying for its restoration before her mother had died, would be sad but wonderful, too. Her mother's legacy as a preservationist in New England had now been expanded across the ocean, and that thought brought her smile back and her thoughts completely away from Enzo Affini.

Really. She wasn't going to think about him again. Period.

A renewed pep in her step took her down narrow stone passageways in front of colorful homes, over numerous charming footbridges, then across the *piazza* toward the well-marked clinic she'd be working in for the next four months. When she opened the wide glass door, a bell chimed. Inside, a friendly-looking, middle-aged woman sat at a rather spartan desk. Aubrey had been told most of the people here could speak English, but wouldn't they appreciate it if she tried a few of the Italian phrases she'd learned?

"Buongiorno. Mio nome e Aubrey Henderson. Um...sono qui...per lavorare."

She struggled to remember more, then abandoned the effort when she saw the quizzical and amused expression on the poor woman's face. Doubtless she was completely butchering the pronunciation.

"I'm a nurse with the UWWHA, assigned to the clinic here starting today."

"Welcome. We've been expecting you. And let's speak English, shall we?" said the woman, her smile widening.

"That sounds good." Aubrey smiled back. "I'm working on the language, but I'm not too good at it yet, obviously! I'm hoping by the end of the time I'm here, I'll be practically fluent."

"Learning a language takes time, but working with patients will teach you much. I am Nora, and you can ask me for anything as you need it, *sì*? Come with me." She stood and gestured to the door behind her. "I'll show you where you can put your things. We have a small staff here—you may already know we have just one doctor and nurse working each day, which sometimes gets very hectic. The doctor who is director of the clinic is here today, and he will be the one to show you around. A patient is here right now, though, so the doctor may not be available for me to introduce you at the moment. When you see him, can you introduce yourself? I must greet patients as they arrive, you see."

"Of course. And I confess I don't really know much about how the clinic runs," Aubrey said as she followed Nora down a brightly lit hallway. "I saw the opening in Venice and jumped at the chance to work and explore here." Had jumped at the chance to explore a certain unbelievably sexy prince, too. Except she wasn't thinking about him ever again.

The place was very modern and scrupulously clean. Aubrey glanced into a few rooms to see each had a blue and white examination table, along with the usual medical necessities that you'd see in the United States. Not exactly plush and comfy-looking, but they'd do the job.

Nora opened a tall cupboard door made of the same white material as the rest of the built-in furniture in the space. "Here is a locker for your things, with your uniform inside. I don't see the doctor, so make yourself comfortable and he will be with you soon. Okay?"

"Okay." Nora left her alone and Aubrey was about to put her purse inside the locker until she wondered if maybe she was supposed to change into her uniform right then. Probably yes, since she assumed she would be working with patients right away? Why hadn't she asked Nora those things while she was still here?

Aubrey nearly went back out to the reception area but decided that was silly. If she got into uniform and it turned out to be just an introductory day, it was no big deal. At least she'd be ready, right?

Finding a bathroom, she changed into the crisp white dress, smiling at how it was oddly old-fashioned compared with what nurses wore in the US today, and yet the whole place felt ultramodern. She dropped her clothes and purse into the locker, then hovered around, not sure what to do next. The various drawers and cupboards tempted her to open them up and poke around on her own, but she figured it would be more polite to wait until she was invited to do that.

She stood there for a good ten minutes, and each minute that dragged on felt more awkward. And didn't it make sense to acquaint herself with where things were, in case she needed to take care of a patient sooner rather than later? But luck being the way it was, just as she opened one of the cupboards above the long countertop a deep voice spoke from behind her.

"*Buongiorno.* You must be the new nurse from the US."

Jumping guiltily, she nearly slammed the cupboard shut and turned with a bright smile. Then her heart completely stopped when she saw who stood there.

Enzo Affini. The man who'd unfortunately kept

coming to mind since she'd returned to Venice. The man whose hands and mouth had been all over her two months ago. The man who hadn't bothered to call her again after that very intimate night together.

Aubrey felt a little as if she might just fall over, as though she'd been physically struck at the surprise of seeing him right there in front of her. She barely noticed the elderly man standing next to him as Enzo's dark eyes met hers for several breathless heartbeats. He recovered from the shock more quickly than she did, moving next to her to get something from the cupboard she'd just been snooping in, then turning to the elderly man with instructions. Aubrey didn't hear a word he said, feeling utterly frozen as she watched Enzo and the patient move down the hallway, with Enzo opening the door to the reception area for him, then following behind.

Aubrey sagged against the countertop, her hand to her chest, trying to breathe. Did she have any chance of slipping out the back door before he came back? Though if she did, what would that accomplish? She'd come to Venice to work. Was it her fault that he, incredibly, worked at this clinic, too? Gulping down the jittery nerves making her feel numb from head to toe, she forced herself to stand as tall as possible and stared at the door, willing herself to look calm and confident.

Proud that she managed to be standing there in a normal way when the door opened again... assuming he couldn't see her knees shaking... she met his gaze. The look on his face was completely different than the last time she'd seen him, which was the night they'd parted in the wee hours of the morning. Then, his eyes had been filled with warmth, his sensuous lips smiling and soft.

These lips could have belonged to someone else. Hard and firmly pressed together. His silky eyebrows formed a deep V over his nose as he stared at her.

"Aubrey. To say this is a surprise is an understatement. How did you know I work here?" His voice was a little hard, too. Ultra-chilly. She'd have to be dense as one of the posts sunk into the silt of the lagoon if she couldn't read loud and clear that he was not pleased to see her *at all*.

Something painful stabbed in the region of her heart, but the nervousness and, yes, hurt filling her gut slowly made way for a growing anger at the strange suspicion in his eyes. As if she'd come here on purpose to stalk him or something. "I didn't. I didn't even know you were a doctor. Something you conveniently forgot to mention."

"You knew Dante is a doctor."

"So that meant you had to be one, too? From the way you talked about the restoration of the old homes here, I thought you were an architect or in the construction business or something. You at least knew I was a nurse traveling with Shay." She wasn't about to add that her attraction to him and excitement about deciding to let herself enjoy a little carnal pleasure on the trip had been foremost in her mind, not the thought of what he did for a living, since right now *he* clearly had other things on his mind. Like being ticked off that she was there.

Well, he wasn't the only one feeling beyond annoyed right then. It was painfully obvious that he'd never planned to contact her when she was back in Venice, and she wasn't sure if she was angrier at him for that, or at herself for wishing he'd wanted to.

"I assumed you were working at the hospital with Shay."

"Well, you assumed wrong, the same way I did." She tipped her chin and stared him down, her chest pinching tightly at the way he was looking at her. As if she were some black rat that had scurried out of the sewer into his clinic.

A long slow breath left his lips as he stuck his hands in the dress pants that fitted him as impeccably as the ones he'd taken off as fast as possible the last time she'd seen him. His white lab coat was swept back against his hips, and even through his dress shirt his strong physique was obvious. The body she'd gotten to see in all its glorious detail.

The jerk.

"Our time together before was…nice, Aubrey. But this is a problem."

Nice? The most incredible sexual experience of her life had been *nice* for him? "Why?" she challenged, beyond embarrassed and steaming now. "You're obviously a man who enjoys women. I enjoyed our night together, too. But that's long behind us. Now we move into a professional relationship, which won't be a problem for me at all."

Liar, liar, pants on fire, her inner self mocked. Though maybe it was true. Right now, if he tried to kiss her, she just might punch him in the nose.

"Listen." He shoved his hand through his hair. "I think it's better if we look at other options."

Other options? The rise of panic in her chest shoved aside her anger with him. Nora had said he was director of the clinic. Did that mean he could toss her out if he wanted? She knew there weren't any positions available at the hospital. What if there wasn't a single other place to work in all of Venice?

"Enzo, there's no reason we can't work through this. I—"

"Dr. Affini." Nora rushed into the hallway with a boy who looked to be about seven trailing behind. Blood stained his torn pants and dripped onto the floor with every step he took. "Benedetto Rossi is here. He fell off his bike. I tried to call his father and his *nonna* but haven't reached either of them. I'll keep trying."

"All right." Instantly, the frown on Enzo's face disappeared, replaced by a calm, warm smile directed at the boy. "Were you taking the corners too fast again?" he asked in English.

The boy responded in quick Italian, gesturing wildly and looking panicked. Enzo placed his hand on the boy's shoulder and led him to an examination room as the boy talked, his head tipped toward the child as he listened. Aubrey hurried to follow. Enzo might not want her here, but maybe she could prove he needed her anyway.

The boy stopped talking to take a breath, and Enzo took advantage of the brief break in his recitation. "Sit up here." He swung the child up onto the exam table. "And speak English, please. I know your *papà* likes you to practice, and the nice nurse here is American. I'm going to take a look, okay?"

Benedetto nodded and sucked in a breath as Enzo leaned over to carefully roll back the boy's ripped pants. The skin beneath sported a wide, bleeding abrasion. It was a nasty one, to be sure, but at first glance it didn't look to be deep enough to require stitches. Not that his leg couldn't still be fractured in some way.

Time to show how competent and vital to this clinic she could be, right? Before Enzo booted her out the door for having *nice* sex with him?

Aubrey shoved down the anger and worry and stab of hurt still burning in her chest and opened a few drawers. Pulled out the supplies she'd need to stop the bleeding, washed her hands, and snapped on gloves. "That's an impressive scrape you've got there," she said to the child, smiling to relax him. And herself, if she was honest. She was glad Enzo had asked the boy to speak English, because she hadn't been able to understand a single word he'd said. "You're obviously a very tough guy. Is your bike okay?"

"No." The panicked look came back. "The wheel is bent, and the tire is flat. *Papà* is going to be angry."

"Oh, surely he won't be angry when he sees you were hurt," Aubrey said.

"Yes, he will." He licked his lips and turned his wide-eyed attention back to Enzo. "Nonna will be, too. I was supposed to be getting bread and *seppioline*, but I went to play with Lucio first. And then I fell off my bike near his house."

"Let's worry about that later." Enzo straightened to send the boy another wide smile he should patent to relax a patient. Or kindle some other reaction, depending on the circumstances and who he was sending it to. "First, we're going to stop the bleeding. Then we'll take an X-ray to look inside your leg. Luckily your *papà* signed papers allowing me to treat you the last time you were here."

"X-ray?" Tears sprang into the boy's eyes. "You think my leg might be broken?"

"I don't think so, no. But we'll check just to be sure." Enzo patted the child's shoulder and glanced at Aubrey as she cleaned the wound. "Looks like you have that under control. I'm going to get the portable X-ray."

"Yes, Doctor," she said, oh, so coolly and professionally, staring at the boy's leg because she didn't want to look at Enzo's wickedly handsome face. Be distracted by all his undeniable beauty, and get mad at him all over again.

He returned just minutes later, rolling the cart to the table. "Between the blood and rips, I'm afraid these pants are ruined, Benedetto. I'm going to cut them off so we don't have to slide them down over your leg."

"What? How will I get home without pants?"

"We keep spare clothes here for things just like this. No worries, okay? Nurse Aubrey here will find you something. Now, this won't hurt at all, and you'll get to see a picture of your bones afterward, which I think you'll like."

Enzo was so incredibly gentle as he lifted the child's leg to place the X-ray plate under his calf, her vexation with the man softened slightly. The steady stream of calm, amusing conversation he kept up with the boy actually had the child laughing, which was a dramatic difference from the scared tears of earlier. She had to grudgingly admit that the man had a wonderful bedside manner. In more ways than one, darn it.

Enzo straightened, and his dark eyes lifted to hers. "This will take just a short time to develop."

"I'll wait to dress the wound until you've taken a look. Then find those pants you talked about. Unless you want to wear the ones I brought, Benedetto? They have little flowers on them—quite pretty."

"Eww, no!" He obviously knew she was kidding, because he laughed, and the impish smile she'd so enjoyed on Enzo's face the first moment she'd met him returned as he winked at her.

"Benedetto wearing flowered pants to the fish market just might make the fishermen's day, don't you think, Aubrey?"

"I don't want to wear them, but I want to see you in them, Nurse Aubrey! I like flowers on girls' clothes."

A laugh left Enzo's annoyingly sexy lips, and

the eyes that met hers held a hint of the amused look she remembered too well. "You're smart for being so young. Very, very smart. I'll be right back."

Hopefully this proved they could take care of patients and interact just fine, and the weight in Aubrey's chest lifted a little. She absolutely did not want to have to leave Venice before she'd learned more about how her mother's foundation could help restoration projects there. Before she'd barely had a chance to explore this unique city. Enzo Affini might be superficially charming and very irksome, but she was confident she could look past all that and think about him in a strictly professional way while she worked here.

She could and she would.

Aubrey chatted with the child until Enzo returned, and she quickly looked away from him, because every time she let her gaze run over his dress shirt and doctor coat she remembered the strong body, smooth, tanned skin, and soft dark hair on the muscular chest beneath it all. Which made her feel a little warm, and while she wanted to think it was her anger bubbling up again, she knew the ridiculous truth.

Mad at him and hurt by him and needing to keep her distance from him didn't seem to affect being *attracted* to him one bit. What in the world was wrong with her?

"Good news, Benedetto. No fracture." Enzo's voice warmed the whole sparse room. "So Nurse Aubrey is going to get you bandaged up while I go take a look at your bike. See if I can fix it so it's good as new. Is it outside?"

"Sì." The boy's eyes lit in surprised excitement. "Can you do that?"

"I'm going to give it a try. Aubrey, when you're done, please get a tube of topical antibiotic from the drawer for his *papà* to pick up later when he comes back for us to change the dressing. And will you look in the cupboard next to yours to see if there are any pants that would work for him?"

"Of course." She watched his tall frame leave the room, completely failing in her determination to not admire that beautiful dark hair and his broad shoulders and the elegant way he moved.

Ugh. She quickly turned back to Benedetto. Being sweet to this child and fixing his bike didn't erase the reality that the man had virtually accused her of hunting him down just moments ago. A Jekyll and Hyde type, to be sure.

When she had the boy's leg securely bandaged, she stood and smiled. "I'm going to look for those pants. Be right back."

The first cupboard had a neatly stacked pile of all kinds of clothes, but after fishing through them she couldn't find a single pair of pants. The one next to it had what looked like running shorts and a few T-shirts, and a lone pair of gray sweatpants. More searching proved there was nothing else around, so she took the sweatpants back to the exam room, dug into her purse for her sewing kit, and showed the child the pants. "This is the best I can do, I'm afraid. They're way too big for you, but I'm going to make them fit as best I can. Okay?"

"Okay." He eyed them doubtfully. "How can you make them fit? They are huge."

"Ah, I have many talents, young man. You just

wait. Can you stand up without it hurting too much?"

She helped him from the table and held the pants up to his waist. They draped a good foot and a half onto the floor, and she made a pencil mark. Then she took scissors from the drawer, cut off the bottom half of the legs, then cut into the elastic waistband. Removing a big chunk of fabric, she then stitched it back together as the boy patiently watched.

"Eccoli!" she said, feeling pretty satisfied with her work and her ability to come up with a good Italian word to boot. "Step into them and see if they'll stay on you now."

Once he'd pulled them on, he stared down at the pants, then up at her with a big smile. "They are okay! I didn't think you could. Thank you very much."

"You're welcome. Here's that tube of antibiotic Dr. Affini wants put at the front desk for your dad or your *nonna* to pick up. Now, let's go see how he's doing with your bike."

She tried hard to ratchet back the way her heart

squished as they stepped out to the *piazza*, trying to shore up her negative feelings about the man currently crouched on the stone pavement. His head was bent over the bicycle wheel as he used some kind of wrench on it. He'd taken off his lab coat, and his necktie was askew and tucked inside the buttons of his shirt. Midmorning sunshine gleamed in his hair, and his eyes were narrowed as he concentrated on his task.

"Can you fix it, Dr. Affini?" Benedetto sounded both worried and hopeful.

"Good…as…new. You're going to ride like the wind." One last turn of the wrench, then he stood to pump a little more air into the tire. Obviously pleased, he brushed his hands together, beaming a smile at the boy. "How's your leg feel?"

"Okay. Thank you so much. I'm going to get the things my *nonna* wanted, then go straight home."

"Here are the instructions for your *nonna* and *papà* on when to come back, and later, for changing the bandage again and using the antibiotic ointment." He pulled a folded paper from his pocket, and his eyes met Aubrey's. "You did put the ointment at the desk?"

"I gave it to Nora after we set him up with new pants."

"*Bene.* They—" He stopped short as he looked at the child's pants, then, after a long pause, laughed out loud.

"What?" she asked, bristling that he obviously thought her sewing job was amusing. Or bad. Or something. "There wasn't anything that would fit, so I made a bigger pair fit at least a little."

"I see that. They look very good on you, Benedetto. Very good." He reached to give the child a quick hug. "Now you go run your errands. Come back tomorrow to let us take another look and change the dressing, and ask your *nonna* or *papà* to call me before that if they have questions."

"Okay. I don't think Papà will be as mad now that my bike is fixed. Thank you again!"

Aubrey watched the boy mount the bike and ride it slowly and carefully away, and she smiled. "He's being very cautious now, I see."

"Not for long, I'm sure." Enzo's amused gaze

met hers. "Good thing you made the pants fit so the legs wouldn't get caught in the chain and make him fall again."

"Yes, good thing. So why were you laughing at my sewing job?"

"I wasn't laughing at your sewing job. I was laughing because those are—were—my pants."

Her mouth fell open. "What? They were in the cupboard you told me to look in! With some shorts and T-shirts and…and…" The vision of the neatly folded shorts and manly T-shirts in that cupboard made her voice fade away. Why hadn't she realized those items were all the same size, when the ones in the other cupboard had been a total mishmash? Heat washed into her face. So much for showing she was indispensable around here. "I'm so sorry. Really sorry. I thought—"

"Aubrey." He pressed his fingertip to her lips. "It's fine. Sometimes I run when the clinic's slow, and I keep clothes here for that. Obviously, they served Benedetto well. Between you and me, his father is very old-school and can be hard on him when he makes mistakes. Not having to show up in bloody, torn pants with a broken bike is a good thing."

"What about his mother?"

"She died a few years ago."

Her heart squeezed for the little boy who had lost his mother far too soon. Having her own mother for twenty-seven years hadn't been nearly long enough. She looked into Enzo's eyes and could see they'd shadowed with sadness for the boy, too. Probably for the child's whole family, since he obviously knew them fairly well, and seeing how much he cared melted her heart. Just a little, though. "Poor little thing," she said softly. "It's good that you fixed his bike for him, then."

"And I thank you for making the pants work. We Venetians take care of our own."

Not being a Venetian, she knew he wasn't talking about her, but somehow it felt absurdly nice to be included in the thought. Which reminded her how much she wanted to stay here for the next few months, and how Enzo Affini had implied just a bit ago that he didn't want to work with her in the clinic at all.

"So." She squared her shoulders and looked him in the eye. "We were having an important conversation about my job and future here, and you need to know I'm not leaving."

"No?" His lips quirked at the same time that suspicious frown dipped between his eyes again. "And if the director of the clinic, who would be me, says you have to? That he'll find you employment somewhere else in Italy?"

"I've already worked two months in Rome. And I've come to Venice now because this is where I want to be. Didn't taking care of Benedetto prove we can work together just fine?"

"Aubrey, I cannot promise that I wouldn't allow myself to be seduced by you again."

Her mouth fell open. "I didn't seduce you! I believe it was you who seduced me. And I *can* promise that it won't happen again. I don't even find you attractive anymore." Which was kind of true. For good reason. And yes, her nose was growing a little, but she'd stick with that half-truth if it killed her.

A slight smile softened the hard lines on his

face. "That I know is a lie. Shall we agree that the seduction was on both sides? And that's the problem, because I can't have an affair with someone who works at the clinic."

"Listen. I know we only got together at first that night because you wanted to ask me questions about Shay." Knowing that hadn't kept her from jumping into bed with him, though, had it? "It was just a one-night thing. I have zero desire to...to co-seduce you again."

"And if I can't say the same thing?"

She wondered if he knew he spoke the words in the same low, sexy rumble he'd used when they'd kissed and made love, and she sucked in a breath as memories of all that shimmered between them. "Then that's your problem, not mine. Though you clearly didn't want to anyway, since you never called me in Rome."

Oh, hell. Did those words really fall out of her mouth? Implying she'd wanted him to, and wondered if he would, and hadn't liked that he hadn't? Lord, that was the last thing she'd wanted to admit.

"Aubrey. It wasn't—"

"Skip it." She held up her hand, desperate to stop him from giving her some lame excuse he didn't really mean. "We'll just have to figure out how to work together. I have no doubt we can act like mere acquaintances and pretend that night never happened."

"That would be extremely difficult. For me, at least."

"Uh-huh. And since we're going to have a professional relationship, please stop with that tone of voice and…and those kinds of comments."

"I thought you no longer find me attractive, so why is that a problem?"

The way her heart fluttered and her breath caught at his physical beauty and sexiness and utter male appeal, she knew it would be tough going to learn to be immune to it.

"It's not. Now, I'd appreciate it if you'd give me a tour of the facility, so I'll know where everything is when a patient arrives, Dr. Affini." She moved past him to the clinic door and paused there. "Shall we?"

CHAPTER TWO

ENZO STUDIED THE woman standing there by the door, looking expectantly at him. Coolly, her pretty chin tipped up as her eyes challenged him. Those eyes had seduced him the second he'd met her two months ago, at the same time he'd wondered what her story was, and her friend Shay's, too, who'd shown up in his brother's life pregnant.

He still had no idea if the two women had an agenda that included snagging two doctors who also happened to be princes, and whose problems with their inheritance had been well-documented in the press. He'd planned to just talk with Aubrey the night they'd spent together, but talking and laughing had led to kissing, then touching, which had led to other, more than pleasurable and memorable things he hadn't been able to stop thinking about ever since.

But getting involved with a woman—a woman he wasn't sure he could trust—at the same time he was trying to save his heritage had seemed like a bad idea.

And now here she was, in his clinic, in all her beautiful glory. *Stunned* would be the only word that could describe how he'd felt when he'd seen her standing there, looking sexier than anyone should be able to look in a nurse's uniform. How coincidental was it that she'd just happened to be signed up for employment there?

Too coincidental, as far as he was concerned.

"You working somewhere else makes more sense. I'll make a few phone calls to the hospital and the other clinic. I can't promise to find you a position there but can also look at Verona or Padua for temporary nursing opportunities."

"This is ridiculous." She folded her arms across her chest and stared him down with such laser intensity, a lesser man might have caved right then and there. "You need a nurse here, obviously, or I wouldn't have been hired. I want the job, I'm qualified for the job, and I'm here now ready to work. Did I do well helping with Benedetto?"

"Yes. But that's irrelevant to the problem."

"Are you saying that you're so chauvinistic and weak around women that you wouldn't be able to behave professionally around me?"

"What? Of course not." He couldn't decide whether to laugh, or be irritated, or both. And admit that their night together had happened because he'd been unable to resist being with her then, so yeah, maybe he was weak. "You're pretty sassy for a woman who wants her boss to keep her around."

"And you're pretty insulting, implying I hunted you down in coming to work here." She stepped closer and poked her finger into his chest, her eyes flashing blue-gray fire. "I can show you the letter from the UWWHA confirming my employment here, which is dated long before we met. And I'm not going to let a mistake from two months ago keep me from having this job now. So you're stuck with me, and I'm stuck with you."

He grasped her hand in his, planning to move her finger from his sternum, but found himself curling it against his chest instead. "A mistake, was it? You didn't seem to think so that night."

"That night, I didn't know what I know now." She yanked her hand from his. "And neither did you. So we act like adults and work together like adults. Professional relationship, pure and simple. Now, let's get on with you showing me around here, before more patients show up."

He felt his lips curve, despite knowing that if he agreed to keep her here, it might well be a disaster waiting to happen. He'd been attracted to her smarts and beauty and sense of humor before. Add to that her spunk and tough attitude?

Irresistible.

Dio. He sighed and stepped around her to open the door. "I have a bad feeling the next few months are going to challenge me at a time I have too many challenges already," he said.

"Lead on, Aubrey Henderson. I'll show you the ropes if you promise not to hang me with them."

"I never make promises I'm not sure I can keep," she said in the sweetest of tones, smiling up at him, her eyes filled with victory, flashes of exasperation, and a touch of the teasing look he'd fallen for before. "But I'll do my best, Dr. Affini. That I can promise."

Several days working at the clinic hadn't dimmed Aubrey's enthusiasm for the job, it had made her even more excited about it. Seeing the clinic sign up ahead had her stepping up her pace the same way it had the first day she was there. She was so glad she'd embarked on this adventure, in spite of Enzo Affini's insulting attitude and the uncomfortable tension between them.

Why in the world had she decided to sleep with him that first night she'd met him? What a mistake that had turned out to be! It was so obvious now that she never should have gotten involved with him, especially since she'd known all along that the main reason he'd offered to show her around Venice was because he'd wanted to pick her brain about Shay.

Except she just hadn't been able to resist, fool that she was.

Now, though, she was going to concentrate on work and only work. Thank goodness Enzo hadn't made her go somewhere else, since taking care of mostly tourists was so interesting. In some ways completely different than what she'd done back at home, and in other ways it was exactly the same. And the locals she'd seen so far in the clinic had been a fascinating mix of characters, from charming and sweet to gruff to downright cranky. Though she supposed that would describe all the people in the world—when it came down to it, everyone was much more alike than they were different, weren't they?

She changed into her crisp white dress and glanced in the locker-room mirror. Caught herself thinking about how surprisingly well it fit and how flattering it was and how Enzo just might think so, too, and why did even her simple uniform make her think about the man? Pathetic.

What was wrong with her that she still caught herself feeling doe-eyed over a guy who'd wondered if she was trying to trap him or something?

Cool, professional relationship only. No fighting or kissing allowed. They'd done pretty well with that the past couple days. Surely after a few more it would feel as if their time together before had never happened?

Yeah, right. Whenever they were alone in a room, the low sizzle humming between them was very hard to ignore.

Nora poked her head into the locker room. "I have a British couple here to see the doctor. A Mr. and Mrs. Conway. You want to get started with them first?"

"Of course." She ushered the middle-aged couple to one of the exam rooms. "Hello, I'm Aubrey Henderson, the nurse on staff today. Can you tell me what you're here for?"

"I've been pecked by a bird," the woman exclaimed. "By an awful dirty bird, and it hurts!"

"All right. Let's have a look." Aubrey was about to shut the door for privacy when Enzo appeared, filling the doorway with his big, irritating, masculine presence.

"Mind if I stay?" he asked. His face was impassive, but she could see a glint of amusement in the depths of his dark eyes at the woman's dramatic statement. "I need to evaluate how our American nurse is doing."

"Of course," Aubrey said before the patient could answer. And was that what he really wanted, or was he there to just rattle her again, knowing this was probably not a serious situation? "This is Dr. Affini."

"I'd like to see what the doctor thinks about this!" the woman exclaimed. "I've probably got some disgusting disease."

"Mrs. Conway, why don't you sit on the table here and show me where it hurts? Sir, you can sit in one of these chairs."

"Right on the top of my head, that's where it hurts! Bleeding, too." She held up a tissue with some specks of blood on it, waving it first at Aubrey, then Enzo. "What if I've been exposed to some terrible bird infection?"

Aubrey donned gloves and gently pushed the woman's hair aside to find a small, reddened indentation. "I can see this probably hurts. But I don't think it's too serious. Let me get some antiseptic to clean it with."

"Not too serious? You'll change your mind when I tell you the story." The woman sat straighter and waved her hands. "I'm minding my own business on a park bench in that big main square where the basilica is. Pigeons were walking around, and I pulled a little treat from my purse to give to one. Then this great, giant black bird dive-bombs me from the sky and grabs the treat from the pigeon!"

Aubrey pulled the cotton and antiseptic from the cupboard, and, when she turned, saw Enzo's eyes dancing and his lips obviously working to not smile at the dramatic recitation. Feeling her own mouth dangerously quiver, she quickly turned back to her patient to keep from looking at him. "And then? How did your head get pecked?"

"So I pull another treat from my purse, and the nasty black bird takes it, drops it, then scares me to death when he suddenly flies up, flapping his great wings in my face as he does. Lands there, right on my head! I shrieked, of course, and jumped up, and it pecked me. Hard! Why, I'm lucky it wasn't my eye he put out."

Aubrey glanced at Enzo. Fatal mistake, as his expression clearly showed he wanted to laugh, and a chuckle bubbled in her own chest when she saw how he was struggling.

Turn away. Do. Not. Look. At. Him.

She quickly turned to the woman's husband, who appeared more weary than worried. "Did you see what kind of bird it was?"

"Some black bird. Don't know what kind, I'm not a birdman. Especially Italian birds. Medium sized. Yellow beak, I think." He turned to his wife. "You brought it on yourself, you know. Who gives a pigeon mints to eat? The bird that pecked you was probably so shocked and ticked off, it felt it had a right to attack."

"Well, I never!" The woman looked beyond insulted as she flung her hand toward her husband.

"And this is the kind of support I get after giving him thirty years of my life!"

Oh, Lord. Aubrey held her breath. Dang it, she would have been fine if not for Enzo's unholy grin. She would.

"I... I think I've cleaned it well, Mrs. Conway," she said.

"What do you think, Doctor? Don't you think I may get some nasty infection or disease? A filthy bird in a filthy square full of filthy people is bound to have given me something awful. Don't I need an antibiotic or something?"

Aubrey was impressed at how carefully he looked at the tiny wound, since he knew as well as she did that it was nothing. "Nurse Henderson has done a good job of cleaning it, Mrs. Conway. I'm sure you'll be fine, but if you have any problems with it, be sure to stop back and we'll take another look."

"We're leaving tomorrow anyway. Thank heavens for that. And what a waste of time to come here for help." Looking miffed and completely unsatisfied, she slid off the table, and Aubrey led her back out to the lobby, making sure to not look at Enzo as they passed. The woman's parting words before she walked out the door had Aubrey holding her breath hard again when she went back to the room to be sure it was clean for the next patient.

Enzo appeared again in the doorway. "Ah, she's the kind of patient that makes this job worthwhile. A pick-me-up from the more serious stuff we deal with, don't you think?"

Aubrey couldn't hold it in another second, and she pressed her hands against her mouth to subdue the laugh that spilled out. "That's for sure. You know what she said when she left?"

He folded his arms across his chest. "What?"

"She said, 'What does that doctor know about birds? He's obviously a quack.'"

His sexy laughter joined hers, and she quickly pulled him into the room and shut the door behind them. "Shh! They might have come back for something! What if they hear us?"

"Hear us what?"

She looked up into his eyes, still filled with mirth, but something else, too. That dangerous glint that made her heart flutter and her skin tingle.

She drew in a deep breath. "What is it with you? One minute you're unpleasant, and the next you're throwing out sexual innuendos. Didn't we agree we had to be professional with one another? I think I'm holding up my end here."

"I also said I didn't think we should work together because I knew I'd have problems with that."

Oh, my gosh. Why did he keep saying things he shouldn't in that deep, rumbly voice that sent a warm flush across her skin, reminding her of their first day and night together?

"Enzo." After his name, words seemed to dry up on her tongue and she just stared at him.

"Yes?" He took a step closer. He smelled wonderful, and his body heat seemed to envelop her. He obviously knew what unwelcome thoughts had suddenly crowded her brain, because his gaze settled on her lips.

Which parted involuntarily, and her own small movement toward him that brought her nearly against his chest was completely involuntary, too, and when his arms wrapped around her and his head lowered toward hers all protest and common sense left her mind as her eyes drifted closed in breathless anticipation.

"Dr. Affini? Aubrey?"

Her eyes snapped open to see his, dark and dangerous and full of heat, staring right back at her. Time seemed to halt for several heartbeats until they both managed to gather their wits at the same time. She stepped back as he let her go, his chest lifting in a deep breath.

"Saved by Nora." He stared at her for one more second before turning to open the door.

She watched him disappear into the hall-way, and the air she'd been holding in her lungs whooshed out. She was in so much trouble here. No matter how many times she remembered his suspicions, no matter how often she reminded herself they had to keep a professional distance, she just kept forgetting.

And it clearly wasn't her imagination that he kept forgetting, too.

CHAPTER THREE

ENZO WAS MORE than glad the Restore Venice Association meeting was about to start. That people were finally wandering off to find seats instead of asking him endless questions about the house that was no longer his, talking about how it was going to be ruined if he didn't get it back, and grilling him on what he was going to do to save it.

He sat toward the back of the room, resisting the urge to slouch in his seat to become semi-invisible. And yes, that probably made him a coward. But since he had no real answers yet, having endless conversations about the house that represented the past seven hundred years of his mother's family history, and his own, and how he had to keep it from going under the wrecking ball, made his gut churn.

He pulled the program from the pocket of his jacket and just as he was about to look at the meeting schedule, a flash of something bright blue or green in the aisle near him caught his eye. He looked up to see that the flash of color was a dress on what looked to be a very attractive body, at least from the back. The fabric skimmed the curves of a sexy feminine derriere that swayed slightly as she walked.

Who was she? He knew most of the people who attended these meetings and definitely would have remembered that body. The woman turned her head to smile at the person standing to let her sit next to him, and Enzo's lungs froze in his chest.

Aubrey.

What the hell was she doing here?

Her silky golden-brown hair skimmed her cheek as she sat, and a slender hand shoved it behind one ear as she dug into her purse for something, coming up with the same program he held in his hand.

He and Aubrey had managed to work together

without fighting, or, worse, kissing, if he didn't count that one near miss yesterday. But now the suspicions about her that had stayed on a low simmer—along with the sexual attraction between them—came bubbling into full boil. First she showed up at his clinic to work, and now she'd decided to come to an art and architecture meeting attended only by Venetians and academics from universities in other countries?

Tourists never came. Neither did many Italians from other areas, because they had their own preservation concerns. And yet here she was, and how was he to believe it was about anything other than her ingratiating herself into his life even more? Doubtless knowing all about his family's problems and the house he loved that she happened to be currently living in.

Did she know he'd owned it before and had rented it out to the UWWHA as he'd planned its renovation? Know that his father had sold it out from under him, and it was about to be resold at a profit? Was renting it from the UWWHA part of her plan somehow?

Enzo's blood ran cold. If Aubrey was trying to charmingly, spunkily wiggle her way into his life, did that mean Shay had done the same thing with his brother? Was there any way this could be another big coincidence?

Seemed incredibly unlikely, but suspicion without proof just festered, and Enzo had enough to worry about right then. So the only solution was to be brutally frank with Aubrey. To ask her some hard questions, and hopefully be able to figure out if she was being honest with him or not. Which might be very difficult, considering he'd had to consciously fight being attracted to her seeming sweetness and smarts and beauty every hour they'd worked together the past few days, but he had to give it a try.

Barely paying attention to the speakers and conversation, Enzo sat through the first half of the meeting trying to decide if he should tackle Aubrey during the break, or wait until it was over. Feeling on edge, he was still pondering that question during the break when the decision was made for him.

A flash of color had him turning from the coffee stand in the front hallway to see her marching right up to him, a militant expression on her beautiful face.

"Just so you know, I had no idea you'd be here today."

"No?" The woman must be a mind reader. "Then why are you here?"

"Because I'm interested in Venice's future. In the restoration of its buildings and artwork."

"So you know nothing about my current situation." He said it mockingly, and she frowned at his tone.

"What situation? Unless you're referring to having to work with me, which you've made more than clear is something you'd rather not do."

"I've seen you're a woman who says what she thinks. So I'm just going to come right out and tell you what I'm thinking. Which is that it's really bizarre that Shay shows up announcing she's pregnant with Dante's baby, and within days she's married to my brother. Then you and I get together, and two months later you magically show up at my clinic to work." He set his coffee down and folded his arms across his chest. "And now you claim to have an interest in the restoration of Venice's buildings, which...shockingly...is my passion, too."

She stared at him, an even deeper frown creasing her brow. "I'm not following."

"Then let me be clearer." He stepped closer, hoping to intimidate her and make her come clean. "What I'm saying is that I can't help but wonder if you and Shay researched Dante and me, and decided two doctor princes would be a nice catch, then figured out how to weasel your way into our lives."

"What?" Her mouth fell open in a gasp. "You have an ego the size of Mount Vesuvius, you know that? I'm not even going to dignify that accusation with an answer. You can believe what you want to believe. But if you think insulting me is going to get me to leave the clinic, you've got another think coming. I'm staying until my contract is over, so just deal with it. And you're going to feel pretty ridiculous when you realize your fantasies of me wanting to trap you into something were all in your own small mind."

She spun away and stalked off, and he stood there long seconds just watching that sexy behind of hers until she went through the doorway to the meeting room again.

He let out a long breath. Maybe his strategy had backfired this time. But if she and Shay weren't what they seemed, he had to believe that, sooner or later, one of them would tip their hand and the truth would come out.

The president of the association spoke in English as he opened the second half of the meeting. The back of Enzo's brain absently noted that there must be university guests from other countries for this portion of the presentation and discussion. Then his focus snapped big-time to the speaker when the next words out of the man's mouth were a name.

Aubrey Henderson.

What the...? He sat up straighter to watch her stand and make her way to the lectern, noticing that plenty of the men in the room seemed to be admiring her swaying walk as much as he had been earlier. Until he'd been shocked to see whose enticing body was wearing that dress.

"Two years ago, Ms. Henderson graciously adopted the renovation of the large fresco depicting angels and warriors in one of the churches at San Sebastiano. The twenty-five thousand dollars she donated have brought this art treasure back to life, and we encourage all of you to visit and admire it. In recognition of this gift, we present this plaque to show our appreciation."

Applause greeted Aubrey as she accepted the plaque, then stood with the president as photos were snapped. If he'd been surprised before, this time Enzo could barely wrap his brain around what he was witnessing.

Aubrey had donated money to a restoration project in Venice? Two years ago? And not just a little money, but a very nice chunk—enough to completely pay for that project, which was one of so many beautiful old masterpieces in Venice that needed repairs.

Her smile seemed to light the whole room as

she leaned toward the microphone, holding the plaque to her breasts. "Thank you. I appreciate this recognition, but it was our privilege to be able to adopt the fresco project. My late mother, Lydia Henderson, lived her life working to save old buildings from being demolished instead of renovated. She led numerous architectural review boards in Massachusetts and elsewhere in New England. During her illness, we decided to donate to this project because she was fascinated with the history of Venice and had always been drawn to images of angels and warriors. She often said that all of us had a chance to be both in our lives. I'm proud to say that she truly was an angel and a warrior, and I hope to live my life at least a little bit like she did."

Even from the back of the room, Enzo could see her blinking back tears as she said one more thank you, then headed back to her seat. It seemed she'd taken only a few steps before her gaze lifted to his. Her eyes narrowed and her graceful gait seemed to falter for a moment before she turned her attention to finding her seat again.

Dio. What was he supposed to think now?

He stared at the back of her silky head and had no idea of the answer to that question. But one thing he did know?

He owed her an apology.

Obviously, she had good reason to be at the meeting that had nothing to do with him, and, yeah, she'd been right. He did feel ridiculous that he'd assumed otherwise.

He huffed out a breath, not wanting to have to give her that *mea culpa*, but knew he had no choice. The meeting seemed to drag on forever, his eyes on the back of her head instead of the speaker for most of it. Finally, the crowd stood and he jostled his way through the throng until he was able to catch her just as she was walking out the door.

"Aubrey. Wait. I need to talk to you."

She stared straight ahead across the *piazza*, walking faster. "You've already said plenty, Dr. Affini."

"I want to apologize."

"For what?" She finally turned to look at him,

and if the daggers she was sending from her furious gaze had been real, he'd be lying dead on the pavement. "Accusing me of showing up at your clinic to trap you? Of stalking you at the architecture meeting? Of faking an interest in restoration? You overestimate yourself."

"I know. And I'm sorry. I am. Truly."

"Hmmph." The sound she made wasn't exactly an acceptance of his apology, but at least she slowed down a little, instead of surging through the crowd as if she were in a sprint race.

He reached for her arm to slow her even more and was glad but a little surprised that she didn't yank it loose. "Aubrey. Things are…difficult right now. Which maybe is making me think and act in a way I shouldn't."

"Now, isn't that an understatement."

"So can we put this behind us?" He tugged on her arm to force her to look at him. He wanted to see her soften and forgive him, and why that felt so important, he had no idea, since he still wasn't sure what to think about her.

"I'll do my best." She finally turned to him,

and the blaze in her eyes had thankfully cooled. "But only because I love being here and enjoy working at the clinic. And I'm not going to let you ruin either one of those things for me."

This time, she did pull her arm loose, and without another word she took off at a fast pace again. He slowed and decided to let her go. Time to think up a new strategy on how to handle beautiful and mysterious Aubrey Henderson.

"Stop being negative. We still have time," Enzo said to his accountant and fellow preservationist, Leonardo. Not sure if he was trying to convince Leonardo or himself, he paced the upper floor of the one home he had left in his possession in Venice, staring unseeingly at the finely woven antique carpet covering the *terrazzo* floor. "I'm working on raising more money for the purchase and have also liquidated some assets, which you'll see transferred to the account in a few days. Almost all our vineyards had a good harvest, with more grapes sold this year to other wineries than last, and our own vintages are selling well. Dante gave me the numbers a few days ago. It's coming together."

At least, he hoped it was. His gut tightened at how much money he still needed to buy back the childhood home he loved, but he was determined to make it happen.

"But the new owner told me he expected the sale to the hotel chain to go through within the next three weeks," Leonardo said.

"Which gives us two and a half to beat them to it."

"I was looking through all the photos of the house you gave me. Whether the sale goes through or not, I'll need more of the exterior, the internal courtyard, and the bedrooms to provide to the commission proactively, so they'll agree to a six-month delay of the interior demolition the hotel is planning. Buy us some time to convince the commission to refuse to allow it. If the sale ends up going through to the hotel, maybe they'd end up selling it back to you if they can't remodel it the way they want to. So can you get those for me?"

"Yes." Or at least, he hoped he could. He might not be the one who owned and rented the property to the UWWHA anymore, but he did know a certain beautiful, questionable tenant living there. If she wasn't so angry she refused to talk to him anymore, let alone allow him in the house. "I'll get them to you as soon as possible. *Arrivederci.*"

Familiar burning anger swelled in Enzo's chest as he hung up, but he fought it down. Holding close the bitterness and fury he felt was a distraction he couldn't afford. Despising his father and his selfish actions didn't change a damn thing.

No, Enzo just had to work harder and outbid the hotel chain. That was all there was to it.

Thinking of the house had his thoughts turning to Aubrey again. He could picture her sleeping in one of the run-down but still beautiful bedrooms, her shining hair spread across the pillow. Curled up reading a book in a chair in front of one of the massive stone fireplaces. Wandering the halls admiring the amazing rooms and artwork and antiquities.

He dropped into a chair to stare out over the Grand Canal. *Confused* was probably the best word to describe how he felt about her. Along with suspicious and extremely attracted.

Were she and Dante's lover—no, wife, now—two women with an agenda? So many things pointed to *yes, maybe*. Then again, there was something so appealing, so seemingly genuine about Aubrey, something that drew him to her in a way that he couldn't quite remember happening with another woman. He'd seen it when she'd cared for Benedetto, then fixed up Enzo's pants for the child, which made him chuckle all over again. And a number of other times as they'd taken care of patients together.

Yet there were all those coincidences that made it hard to believe she was for real.

So where did that leave him?

The same place he'd always been. Still planning to save his inheritance here and in Arezzo a different way. Through hard work. Still planning to never marry, regardless of what that meant to the future of the properties that should be his.

Except Aubrey didn't know that.

Feeling oddly unsettled, he decided to give Dante a call. Between his brother's new wife and his always busy job as a trauma surgeon, Enzo hadn't seen the man in weeks. He hoped that meant everything was reasonably fine, but he wanted to hear that for himself. With any luck he'd be available to talk, and not in the middle of surgery, and Enzo was glad Dante picked up after only two rings.

"To what do I owe the honor of hearing from my brother, since you haven't called me for weeks?" Dante said in his ear.

"The phone works both ways, you know. I figured you were busy with Shay and didn't want to bother you."

"You've been bothering me your whole life, so why change things now?"

"Point taken." The smile in his brother's voice made Enzo smile, too. "How's work?"

"Busy. So busy that we haven't been able to get back to Arezzo for a while, but we plan to soon. How about you?"

Hearing his brother say "we" when it came to his life and travels sounded so strange, but, with a baby on the way, he'd be saying that for the rest of his life, wouldn't he? Something everyone would have to get used to. "Busy, too. Always is during the heavy tourist season, as you know. How's Shay? Feeling all right?"

"She's well. Getting more round, but feeling good."

Why the conversation felt so awkward to him, Enzo wasn't sure, but he sensed that his brother wasn't feeling awkward at all. He sounded happy, maybe? Excited? Enzo hoped so, and also hoped his brother's heart wasn't going to get mashed up over all of it. "Glad to hear it. Well, I just wanted—"

"What's the situation with the house?" his brother interrupted. "Last time we talked you were having trouble raising enough funds."

"Still working on it." No point in adding to his brother's concerns, since they'd already collaborated to borrow as much as possible against their wineries.

"I heard that Aubrey Henderson is back in Venice with the UWWHA and living at your house now."

"It's not my house anymore, remember?"

"It will always be your house." Dante's voice was fierce. "I'm still exploring a few other possibilities for raising money, and I know you're going to find some way to buy it back. No one is as determined as you when you set a goal for yourself."

"Thanks. And I am determined." Somehow, his brother's vote of confidence eased the tightness in his chest a little, even if they were just words and not money in the bank.

"So how's it going with Aubrey working at the clinic, or shouldn't I ask?"

"How did you hear about that?"

"You know how women like to talk," his brother said drily. "I heard it from Shay. But she didn't have to tell me you went out with Aubrey. I had a gut feeling you'd end up in bed with her when you told me you were going to introduce yourself to ask questions about Shay. Despite my telling you I knew the child was mine."

His brother's voice was chiding, but he didn't sound annoyed with him anymore. But who wouldn't have wanted to find out more about the woman his brother wanted to marry? "Maybe your gut feeling was just indigestion."

"Or not. Aubrey's a beautiful, smart woman and I knew you wouldn't be able to resist. And neither would she. If there's one thing the Affini men are good at, it's charming women, right?"

"I hope we have more going for us than that, since it's one of the many things about our father that we both despise."

"Yeah." Dante's joking tone disappeared. "Listen, I just got a surgery consult. Thanks for calling, and I'll talk to you soon."

Enzo stood to shove his phone in his pocket, sling his camera around his neck, and grab the keys to his boat. He jogged down the curved stone staircase of one of the several homes that had been in the Affini royal family for centuries.

It struck him that the way to find answers to his

questions about Aubrey seemed obvious. What was that old saying? Keep your friends close and your enemies closer? He had no idea if Aubrey was friend or foe, but keeping his distance from her wasn't the answer, since he couldn't feel good about making her leave the clinic and find a job somewhere else, especially now that her wanting to be in Venice might be partly because of her late mother. He understood that kind of loss, and if staying here helped Aubrey heal a little, she should have that chance.

And hopefully, spending time with her both at work and socially would eventually tell him the truth.

If he could keep his damned libido out of the picture, that was. Keeping the enemy close was one thing. Sleeping with the enemy? That was something he was sure never ended well.

It was handy that he was the one who drew up the clinic work calendar. That allowed him to be sure to have her time off scheduled for when he wanted it to be, and the thought made him smile for reasons he shouldn't be smiling. Before he started the motor to his boat, he pulled out his phone again. The sound of her answering with a cheerful hello on the other end of the line made him smile even more, and he shook his head at himself. Hadn't he just reminded himself moments ago that he had to keep an emotional distance from her?

If just the sound of her voice made him smile, that wasn't going to be easy. Though he had a feeling that smile would go away quickly when she learned it was him calling.

"Aubrey, it's Enzo. I was wondering if by chance you were at the house you're renting. I need to get inside to take a few photos."

CHAPTER FOUR

"Take a few photos?" Aubrey's voice in his ear sounded beyond surprised. "What do you mean?"

"I'll explain when I see you. If you're available?"

"Why should I be? Oh, wait, it's because I'm trying to snag a prince doctor for another notch on my bedpost."

"That's not exactly what I said."

"That's right. It actually was that I'm trying to *weasel* my way into your life. Because I'm cunning and deceitful and...and squirmy."

"But you're a beautiful squirmy weasel." He couldn't help it, something about her outrage made him want to tease her even more, though he could hardly blame her for being angry about all he'd said. "If I apologize again, will you let me take the photos?"

"I'll consider it, if it's a good apology and you tell me why you need the photos."

"I apologize for being suspicious of you and your motives." He wouldn't share that he still was. "And I'll tell you when I get there."

"Well, I'm not there right now. I just finished lunch and am outside the restaurant."

"Where?"

"I don't know, exactly. I'm a little lost, to be honest."

He could picture her face scrunched up in thought the way it did at the clinic sometimes. "What's the name of the restaurant?"

"It's called…um… Trattoria da Agnolo. It's off some *piazza*, a little way from a small canal."

He had to chuckle at her description. "Everything is just a little way from a small canal in Venice, or off some *piazza*, but I know where you are. Walk back to the canal. I'll pick you up and drive you back to the house."

"Drive? What do you mean?"

"Drive in Venice means by boat. I thought you said you'd done your homework?"

"If you want me to let you in the house, you'd better be extra, super nice, Dr. Affini, to make up for being so nasty to me."

"I'm not going to be nasty anymore. But I don't have to be super nice, either, because your employment at the clinic is in my hands, remember?"

"And you might remember that the UWWHA has very strict rules about the conduct of the health centers that employ their nurses. They don't like doctors who insult us and try to lord it over us."

Her words pulled a chuckle from his chest that he couldn't hold back. The woman was such an attractive mix of smart and spunky, and he wondered if she knew it. If all that was designed to sucker unsuspecting men into falling for her before she snagged them in her net, or if she really was as wonderful as she seemed. "I'll be there in five minutes to pick you up."

"No, that's all right. I can find my way back to the house. I'm pretty sure it's not too far. I'll just meet you there."

"I'm happy to—"

"No," she interrupted, and her voice sounded nearly panicky. Surely she didn't think he'd fire her if they spent time together that wasn't strictly professional? Then again, he'd said some pretty unpleasant things, so he couldn't exactly blame her for wanting to keep her distance.

He maneuvered his boat through the canal, and as he approached the house he looked for her. Even with a number of people walking on both sides of the canal in front of his house—correction, *formerly* his house—he spotted Aubrey instantly. The golden highlights in her shiny brown hair caught the early-afternoon sunshine, and her gorgeous body wore a sundress that stopped a few inches above her knees, showing off her shapely legs. The sound of his motor must have caught her attention, because she turned, then instantly sent him a half scowl. The boat skimmed to a stop in front of her, and he stood to grab a wooden post to steady the boat and tie it.

"Ciao. Thanks for letting me come by," he said

as he climbed onto the walkway to stand next to her.

"I'm still mad at you. But I confess I'm curious why you want to take photos here. Do you have some connection to this house?"

He looked down at her, wondering how much he should share. How much she might already know. Since the sad and infuriating truth was public knowledge at this point, he didn't see a reason to try to keep it a secret.

"I do. I'll tell you about it as I take the photos."

Aubrey concentrated on carefully putting the old, intricately forged key into the lock and turning it this way and that, her tongue cutely poking out of the side of her mouth as she did. It had been tricky to manage for as long as Enzo could remember, and he couldn't help but tease her about it.

"For a woman so good at creating a small pair of pants from a large one, you seem to be having some mechanical difficulties."

"It's hard to open. I swear I've stood out here five minutes every time—why doesn't whoever rents this house to the UWWHA put on a new knob and lock?"

"It's important to keep the original hardware and historic charm when possible. I thought you said you were a preservationist."

"I am. And you're right." She huffed out a frustrated breath. "I need to have the kind of relaxed attitude the ancient Venetians had, instead of my twentieth-century hurry-up impatience, don't I?"

"Yes." He reached around her, his arm skimming against her warm skin, to take the key from her hand. He inserted it again, and, with a quick turn to the left, the lock clicked and the door swung open.

She stared up at him. "How did you do that?"

"Magic fingers." He wiggled them at her, and she frowned.

"Huh. I don't want to think about the various times you use that line. And what you might be referring to."

"What do you think I might be referring to?" They stepped inside the large entryway, wide sunbeams striping the *terrazzo* floor from every west-facing window. He knew exactly what her words made him think of, and he found himself leaning close to her. A little test to see if she'd take it as an opportunity to start flirting with him again. "Are you remembering our night together?"

"No." Pink tinged her skin. "I just figured a guy like you enjoys making sexual innuendoes to either make women feel uncomfortable, or to think bad thoughts."

"And which are you experiencing at the moment?"

With her hands on her hips, she took a quick step left and frowned up at him. "Listen. You can't be all nasty and accuse me of stalking you, then the next day come on to me. We agreed that if we're going to work together, we need to keep our distance. Treat one another professionally. So tell me why you want to take photos of this place, and how you're connected to it."

He didn't want to talk about the dire situation he faced, but he might be able to tell if she already knew. "Do you know that this place is close to being sold to a large hotel chain? Afterward to be gutted of everything historic except its exterior and turned into a modern hotel?"

"What? That's terrible!" The surprised dismay on her face seemed real. "How can that be allowed?"

"We live in a democracy, and, while we have architectural rules in place, the economics of Venice are a worrying reality. More and more tourists, fewer residents. Many of us are trying to reverse that to some degree, but it's a complicated and difficult task. A lot of houses are now empty, some even slated for demolition. The cost is great to restore them, and when you do you must have someone who can afford to live there."

"I saw in the meeting that there's an architectural review board that a hotel chain or whoever has to go through for permission to tear up a house like this one. It's so incredibly beautiful, I can't imagine it."

His heart warmed at her words, even as he wondered again if she already knew all the truth about it. "It's in great disrepair, as I'm sure you've seen. At times, even some of the tenants working with the UWWHA have complained about the bathrooms, the broken flooring, the peeling frescoes."

"Then they're just stupid," Aubrey said hotly. "If they can't see beyond superficial things like that to love and adore the amazing handwork of the tiling and *terrazzo* and artwork, the incredible design, the awe-inspiring history of a place like this, they should go work somewhere like the US, where a house just eighty years old is considered historic. Every time I walk in this house, I love it more."

"A woman after my own heart," he heard himself murmur. Then mentally stepped back. Distance, remember? *She may not be who she seems.*

The eyes looking up at him were wide and worried. "So, you said you have a connection to this house? Do you think you'll be able to stop the hotel from gutting it?"

"I'm doing everything I can to prevent them from buying it. Getting it into the hands of someone who will renovate and preserve it the way it deserves to be. Who will live in it and love it for the rest of their life."

"Do you have someone in mind? Someone who wants to buy it?"

"Yes. I do." He looked down at her seemingly earnest face. "That someone is me."

Aubrey blinked up at Enzo in shock. "You're trying to buy this house? But what about the house you live in now? Are you hoping to renovate it, then resell it?"

"No." She watched him move around the spectacular room, absently picking up a vase here and a decorative plate there, which Aubrey had been surprised to see lying around. Surely a few of the tenants might have had sticky fingers, unable to resist taking home an antique "souvenir."

"Then what?"

He turned to look at her, his expression deeply serious. Even pained. "This home has been in my late mother's family since the portal was built in the fourteenth century. The second and third floors were added in the fifteenth century, and the top floor, always my favorite as a child, was built in 1756."

Surprise left her staring for a long moment. "So you visited family here as a child?"

"I lived here as a child. Grew up in this house from nearly the day I was born. Of all the properties my family has owned, this one means the most to me. My father kept mistresses in a few of the homes belonging to his side of the family. Always claimed it was his right to do with his own properties as he pleased. And he continues to prove he believes that today, selling away what rightfully should belong to Dante and to me, having been held in trust for us. Except my father has control of that trust."

The bitterness in his tone was unmistakable. "This was one of the houses he sold out from under you and your brother." She didn't say it as a question, because the truth of that was obvious, and her chest filled with a mix of emotions. She wasn't sure what they all were, but she knew for certain the main one was anger. A different anger than she'd felt toward Enzo when he'd been so accusatory at the architectural meeting.

This anger was on behalf of a man who had lost the home he obviously loved. Fury that the buyers didn't care at all about it, ready to pass it on to a hotel chain that couldn't care less about destroying its history, wanting only to transform it into a modern, money-making hotel. Disgust and pain swept through her. Sympathy for both men that their father was as selfish, coldhearted, and uncaring about his sons as her own had proven to feel toward her.

"Yes." Intense dark eyes met hers again.

"But if it was your mother's, how did your father have control of it?"

"When they married, she signed over her property to him. I never asked her why, if it was just expected, or if he insisted. I didn't realize what could happen until she was gone, and it was too late. Now I'm doing all I can to get it back."

"I'm glad, then, that I decided to look past your meanness yesterday." She said it to lighten the weight in her chest, at the same time reminding him she hadn't forgotten about it. And that she expected him to be nicer from now on. "What do you need pictures of?"

"I need better ones of the outside, but will do that last, because any changes to the exterior are regulated much more than the interiors are. And, Aubrey?" His serious dark eyes met hers. "I am sorry about yesterday. I should have kept my mouth shut and not let my worries push me to say things I shouldn't. But I need to look after my brother, you know? We've both had our share of women pretending to be attracted to us just because of our titles and profession. Forgive me?"

She found it hard to believe any woman would have to pretend to be attracted to either of them, but she wasn't about to say so. "Yes. So long as it doesn't happen again."

"Thank you." A real smile touched his eyes. "Okay with you if I go to the bedrooms and baths? Then I want to take pictures of the top floor."

"This way." She started to walk, then stopped

to shake her head at herself. "Wait. You know this house a lot better than I do. Lead on, Dr. Affini."

She followed him up the stairs and watched as he snapped photos of some of the incredible things that had amazed her from the second she'd first walked in the place. "I couldn't believe it when I saw the first fresco in the entry. Then about fell over at the sight of all the gilded stucco on the next level. And the art on the ceiling!" She knew she sounded like a little kid in a candy shop, but that was exactly how she felt. "Just like something out of one of the museums I went to in Rome. I never dreamed I'd ever get to live in a place like this. When I heard the UWWHA had a house to rent, I figured it would be some plain, utilitarian thing."

"I'm glad you're enjoying it." His smile was back in all its attractive glory, and the power of that alone made her feel stupidly weak in the knees. "Wanting to share it for a while was part of the reason I first offered it out to rent as I made plans for its renovation, until my father sold it. The house I'm living in now was already in the process of being restored, and being there as much as possible to supervise it all had seemed like the best plan."

"Well, getting to live here for a while is like a dream come true." She realized that was insensitive, since it had been yanked out from under him. "I'm sorry. Here I am going on about getting to live here, and you can't anymore. Which really makes me mad, just so you know."

"Thank you. Makes me really mad, too." His impish smile widened to show his straight white teeth. "And I have to tell you that your American accent and the way you say things is very cute."

"I don't have an accent. Except maybe when I'm trying to badly speak in Italian."

"Oh, you definitely do."

His warm expression made her lungs feel a little squishy and she frowned to hide it. She refused to think about his words and the low, sexy tone he'd spoken them in as they moved up the intricately carved stone staircase. A complete reversal from the hard words he'd flung at her yesterday.

"One of my favorite rooms here is the library," she said, both to distract herself and because it was true. "So huge! And the ceiling is stunning. The bookcases are in remarkably good shape, too. But the windows are quite leaky and let in an awful lot of light that is doubtless damaging the paintings in the ceiling, not to mention being hard on the books. What are your options for replacing those while still making them look original?"

He stopped dead as they reached the next level, staring at her. "I guess you really do have an interest in historic renovation."

"So you truly thought I went to yesterday's meeting just to stalk you?" She folded her arms across her chest. "Like I said, you're unbelievably egotistical. For your information, my mother's passion for restoration is a part of me. And while doctor princes aren't one of my interests, I have lots of other ones. To me, people who don't are boring as heck."

"Which you most definitely are not, Ms. Henderson." Their gazes seemed fused together for long seconds before he moved toward the bedroom she was currently using. Which made her suddenly, horrifyingly, remember that she'd left clothes strewn around, including some personal items she'd rather not have this hunk of a man see, and never mind that he'd seen a whole lot more of her than just her underwear.

She pushed past him and rushed into the room, grabbing clothes up off the floor and from her bed. And why did it have to be this day of all days that she hadn't taken time to make it?

"Um…let me get this stuff out of your photos."

"It looks like you have more clothes out of the drawers and armoire than I have inside mine. But I think you should leave them." The amused eyes meeting hers danced as he reached out with the curve of his finger to hook the pink underwear lying on the bedspread. "I'll be presenting these photos to the Preserve Venice Committee. I suspect they'll be even more interested if I show how people actually live here, don't you?"

"No, I don't." Heat rushed into her face as she snatched her underwear from his grasp. "I don't normally leave my stuff lying around, so I'm really sorry about that."

"Are you kidding? You're apologizing for leaving your underwear and nightwear out?" He picked up her flimsy black gown by the spaghetti straps and held it up to her. His smile faded a little, his eyes darkened, and his voice went even lower than before. "This bedroom was mine as a child. As a teen, I had many sexual fantasies in this room, and, believe me, seeing what you sleep in has made my day almost as much as it would have back then. Problem is, I'll probably be imagining you in it when we're working together tomorrow."

Oh, Lord. There it was, shimmering between them like a hot, bright light. The connection that had drawn her to him from the moment she'd met him. The chemistry that had sent her headlong into his arms and his bed before she'd thought too hard about it.

No doubt he could see exactly what she was thinking and feeling, despite desperately trying to shore up her past anger with him. Because he leaned closer to brush his mouth against her cheek. Slipped it across her mouth, his breath mingling with hers before he pulled away. The sizzling thoughts swirling in her brain were clear on his face, too. Just as she took a step back and started inwardly scolding herself for letting herself think about the annoying man that way, she could see him mentally and physically retreat, too.

"Got to get these pictures taken. Thanks for letting me in to get this done." He slipped the camera off his neck and seemed to concentrate awfully hard on adjusting the lens. "The hotel's supposed to close on the house in three weeks, so you'll be around for the news."

"Good luck. Let me know if there's anything I can do to help." Probably shouldn't be offering, considering everything, but wouldn't anyone feel bad about his situation?

His gaze moved from the camera back to her. If he was trying to put cool and collected between them instead of hot and alive, he failed miserably. Because it looked for all the world as if he was mentally undressing her, and she just couldn't help the quiver her body responded with.

"I think you know that's an offer I can barely resist, Aubrey Henderson." His chest lifted in a long breath, then, as he turned to walk to the next room, she heard him murmur, "Just barely."

CHAPTER FIVE

HOW WAS AUBREY supposed to actually get any sleep in the bedroom she'd unfortunately learned had been Enzo's as a child?

A bedroom he'd apparently slept in from childhood until recently. *Recently* being when he'd decided to rent it for a short time while he renovated his other house, a move his father had apparently taken as a green light to sell the home Enzo loved. Not that it sounded as if the man who was both Enzo's and Dante's father needed any real excuse to steal from his sons.

That awful reality still burned in her gut for both of them. She couldn't even imagine how that must have felt—how upsetting it would have been for Enzo in particular, selling off this house that held centuries of his mother's history, and his own.

Thinking she couldn't imagine how that felt wasn't exactly true, though, was it? She sure knew from painful personal experience how deceitful and self-centered some fathers could be.

Aubrey glanced at her watch, trying to process all the emotions swirling around inside her. Sympathy for Enzo and what he was going through. Annoyance with his weird suspicions and insults. Confusion about why he seemed to run hot and cold with her, which made her determination to keep things professional and stay angry with him none too easy.

Since she had twenty minutes before she needed to be at the clinic, the burning need to talk to Shay about it all conflicted with her worries that she shouldn't bother her friend at this strange time in Shay's life. And was "strange" an understatement, or what? Aubrey could only hope she was doing okay, and wanting to know that, too, prompted her to give in. To stop walking and sit on a warm wooden bench in the *piazza* near the clinic and pull out her cell phone. All kinds of tourists walked by, from young and old couples, to big tour groups, to families, as she soaked in the amazing beauty and sense of community that was Venice. Children laughed and played, pampered dogs on leashes nosed their way around, and pigeons pecked at invisible delicacies from the old stone at her feet as she dialed Shay's number.

"Hello?" Shay's voice came through, strong and vibrant. "Aubrey?"

"Hey, you! I was wondering how you're feeling. How it's going. You okay?"

"Life has certainly taken a new twist for me, but I'm doing all right. You probably remember the past couple months I was feeling really tired, but now I feel great."

"I hope you're taking good care of yourself. Making sure you get plenty of rest and keeping a little easier pace than usual."

"That's what Dante said."

Was Aubrey imagining a smile in her friend's voice? She hoped and prayed that, however things turned out long-term, it would prove to be good for everyone involved, including the little baby Shay carried.

"I'm glad he's taking care of you, and I hope you listen to that resting thing." Now that she felt good about her friend's health and state of mind, she licked her lips to move on to the other subject on her mind. "What's Enzo been like to you? Has he been a jerk?"

"A jerk?" Shay sounded surprised. "No. I've only seen him a couple times, and he was a little cool but not a jerk. Why, has he been nasty to you?"

The way he spoke to her at the meeting had definitely qualified as *nasty*, but his apology for that had seemed sincere. Hopefully. She had to work with the man, after all, and he'd been pleasant yesterday—and the brief brush of his lips on hers had been more than pleasant.

She shook her head in annoyance that she'd let herself enjoy it. "Never mind. We're managing to work together. And by the way, I wanted to ask, did you know that Enzo used to own the house we rented from the UWWHA? That he and Dante grew up there?"

"I did know. Enzo took me there to get my clothes when I moved in with Dante, and told me then. Though he acted kind of stiff and odd about it. I'm not sure how much of that was because of me and the baby and Dante, and how much was about their dad selling off the property."

"I can't believe their father is so selfish and awful." Though she shouldn't have any trouble believing it, considering she'd experienced the same thing for a short time, too.

"I can't, either. And it's such a beautiful house, standing so tall with those small canals on both sides of it. Almost like an island itself, isn't it? I can't imagine how Enzo feels about losing it. And this house that's Dante's? It's amazing, too. Incredible, really."

"Who would have thought you'd meet a prince and marry him?"

"Not me, that's for sure," Shay said. "I don't need anyone to take care of me. At least, I didn't think so until I got involved with someone famous. Who I didn't even know was a prince or famous, and that has sure complicated things. But it's just temporary, you know. We're only staying married for a year. Until the crazy stalker camera people out there forget about me, and when the excitement of an Affini heir is old news. So the baby and I can stay safe."

"It's been that bad?"

"Unbelievable. They practically knocked me over a few times getting pictures." Shay sounded angry, and who could blame her? "I have to admit it was scary, which is the only reason I went along with his marriage suggestion."

Aubrey still found all of it hard to believe, especially their sudden marriage. But since she'd never been in such an odd and difficult situation, she definitely couldn't and wouldn't judge her friend. She moved on to more basic conversation, asking Shay how her work at the hospital had been, and sharing a few of her experiences at the clinic. Yakking with her the way they had in the past had her smiling so much, she nearly forgot to check the time. "Oh, my gosh, it's late!

I've got to get to work now. Don't be a stranger! Call me with any news, promise?"

"I promise. You keep me posted, too, okay?"

"I will. Talk to you soon." Aubrey hung up and stood, feeling so much better now that she'd talked to Shay. Thankfully, she'd sounded pretty good, so Dante must be treating her well. Not that she was surprised, since, despite Enzo's weirdness with her, she'd seen that, for the most part, he was basically a good guy.

Which was such a bland, understated way to describe the dynamic, sometimes-charming, caring doctor Prince, it didn't even come close.

"Aubrey." Enzo moved into the doorway of the clinic room she was tidying, and she looked up. Her eyes locked on his broad chest, then moved up to that absurdly handsome face, and she quickly busied herself with finishing her cleaning before he could catch her absurdly and inappropriately eyeing him.

"Yes?"

"I'm going on a house call. Hotel call, actually,

not too far from here. I may need you. If we get a patient here that needs immediate attention, one of us can come back."

"Okay." Being around a patient and having work to do would be the distraction she needed to get her head on straight. Or at least she sure hoped it would.

"We're going to see an elderly tourist, female, who's been walking a lot the past couple of days, apparently more than she's supposed to. My friend who manages the hotel told me she isn't feeling very well, but doesn't seem in enough distress to warrant a hospital visit. She has a history of congestive heart failure, but of course we'd need to confirm that's what the problem is. The granddaughter doesn't want her walking here, though, so we're going to go to her."

"What do I need to bring? Nitropaste? Lasix?"

"And a little morphine, in case it is congestive heart failure. Blood-pressure unit and cuff, phlebotomy items and an IV line."

She nodded. "I'll have it all ready shortly."

"Thanks. I'll be in my office."

Proud that she'd resisted the urge to watch him leave, Aubrey gathered up the items, put them in a plastic Ziploc bag she found in the cupboard, then found herself glancing in the mirror. Her ponytail was looking a little loose and she pulled the band out, brushing it to tidy it again. She tried to convince herself it was so she'd look professional for the patient, but she shook her head at the stupid reality that it was partly so she'd look good, period.

Even walking briskly along the wide promenade to the hotel, Enzo proved to be a good tour guide, pointing out historic buildings, homes, and hotels and giving a brief history of each. The hotel manager greeted Enzo warmly, was cordial to Aubrey, then ushered them up elegant floral-carpeted stairs to a small but beautifully appointed room.

"Thank you so much for coming," said an obviously American woman about Aubrey's age as she opened the door wide. "I feel bad that my grandma and I may have overdone it walking and seeing the sights. Should have kept a closer eye on her and not pushed it, but Venice is so tremendous that we got carried away." She frowned and glanced at the older woman sitting across the room in a plush, wingback chair. "I didn't want to put her through the ordeal of going to a hospital if we don't have to, but I felt we needed to know if we should be worried or not."

"That's why we're here," Enzo said, introducing himself and Aubrey, and the woman in turn introduced her grandmother. Aubrey could see by the way the younger woman stared at Enzo that she was as dazzled by his easy smile and good looks as Aubrey had been from the second she met him. As every woman on the planet would be, no doubt, if they didn't know what a split personality he had.

He crouched in front of the white-haired woman, who leaned against the back of the chair holding both hands pressed to her chest. "Tell me how you're feeling."

"Short of breath. But it's barely anything. Really. My granddaughter just likes to worry about me."

Aubrey could immediately see that the woman's breathing was a little labored, but Enzo just smiled as though they were having a regular conversation. "Because that's what granddaughters are supposed to do when it comes to their beloved *nonnas*."

"We've had such a wonderful time." The woman's eyes shone, and her wrinkled face smiled broadly. "The basilica—why, it was more incredible than I ever would have dreamed. And going up the tower to see the islands, and the terracotta rooftops of the city! And taking that boat thing down the canal to see the houses along the water—the history! Unbelievable. Seeing Venice in pictures isn't anything close to actually being here, is it?"

"No, it most definitely is not." His smile widened and the way he glanced up at Aubrey made her heart do that annoying, squishy thing again. "You are a woman after my own heart, Mrs. Knorr."

"You're so handsome I'm sure there are lots of women after your heart, young man. I'd heard

Italian men were beautiful, and have seen for myself it's true. And here you're proving it again."

"Thank you. Sometimes it is true that women show up in my life, but they are not necessarily after my heart." Another glance up at Aubrey, this one odd and questioning, and her throat tightened that he obviously wasn't completely over wondering about her. "Does your chest hurt?"

Yes, Aubrey wanted to say, *because of you and your attitude*. But of course she knew he was asking the patient and not her.

"Just a few twinges," Mrs. Knorr said. "Really, I don't want to be a bother. I'm sure I'm fine, and I'm having a wonderful time. Just a little tired."

"Let me take a listen anyway." Enzo pressed his stethoscope against various parts of her chest, his face inscrutable. "May I look at your ankles?"

She stuck out her foot, and he gently tugged her socks down to press his fingers against the obviously swollen flesh. He drew the socks back up before reaching for her hands and the nail beds were clearly purple. Aubrey hadn't listened to their patient's lungs, but it was pretty apparent that heart failure was likely the problem.

Enzo pulled up a chair and sat in front of the woman, looking at her. "Your heart is a little out of rhythm. Does that happen sometimes?"

She nodded as the granddaughter answered. "She's had fibrillation on and off for some time. Takes a heart medicine to control it. And a little water pill in the mornings."

"They work. They do, Doctor." The eyes that had looked so excited before now reflected the worry on her granddaughter's face. "I don't want to ruin our trip and don't want anyone fussing over me. I'll be fine."

"Only the right amount of fussing, I promise." He patted the woman's hand, and the sweetness of the gesture and the warm expression on his face made her own darn heart about go out of rhythm, too. How could the man be beautiful and smart, so incredibly caring, and the best kisser in the Northern Hemisphere at the same time he was so skeptical and wary with her?

"You are having a little congestive heart failure. But I don't think you need to go to the hospital. So here's what we're going to do," he said. "We're going to have you take the water pill three times a day for three days, and see if that helps with the fluid in your lungs. Increase your beta-blocker, too. Don't worry—" more patting and sweet smiling "—I'll write all this down for you. Aubrey is going to take your blood pressure, and we'll see if we need to tweak the medicine for that, as well. Then draw your blood, just to check a few things, like your potassium and sodium, and to make sure you're not anemic. Okay?"

"Okay. That all sounds good." She gave him an obviously relieved smile.

He stood, and Aubrey worked to do as he'd asked while he spoke to the granddaughter. "When are you leaving Venice?"

"We were supposed to leave tomorrow, to go on to Florence, then the Tuscan countryside. But maybe we shouldn't. Maybe we should arrange to go home."

"Can you stay in Venice three more days, so we can look at her again? If she's feeling better,

I don't see any reason why you can't continue your vacation with maybe a couple fewer stops."

"That's what I want to do," Mrs. Knorr chimed in. Aubrey smiled at the stubbornness that suddenly was loud and clear in her voice. She reminded her a lot of Aubrey's nanny, the retired nurse who'd been obstinate and awesome and was the reason she'd decided on that profession. "I love it here. Three more days sounds perfect, and we can just cut a few days off the rest of our trip somewhere else."

"I love it here, too," Aubrey said, hoping to distract her as she drew the woman's blood. "I get to be here for four months, and I know even that isn't going to feel like long enough."

As she capped off the vials Enzo's gaze caught hers. Held. The man was becoming more and more of a mystery, because she had no idea if he was thinking good things or bad things about her, and decided she couldn't worry about it.

As if that were possible. She focused on being efficient as she worked to gather everything up while Enzo wrote down his instructions, going over them with both women again before they left to go back to the clinic.

"You were so good with her, Dr. Affini," she said as they walked. That was matter of fact, right? Just honestly expressing her admiration with his bedside manner. *Oops. No thinking about his bedside manner.* "Are all elderly patients smitten with you?"

"Definitely not." He grinned at her. "I had one lady throw every pillow on her settee at me the second I walked in her house. And older Italian men tend to be the worst patients in the world, believe me. I'm sure you'll experience one or two while you're here."

"Older men in general are the worst patients, if you'll pardon me saying so. Sexist though that might be. You think you'll be cranky in your old age? I mean, crankier than you already are?"

He laughed. "Most definitely. In fact, it's in my genes. Along with other unfortunate traits."

He didn't look as if he was kidding, but she didn't ask what other traits he could be talking about. Keeping it professional. She could do it.

The rest of the day went by in a blur. Aubrey felt downright exhausted after the influx of patients they'd taken care of all day. Everything from tourists who got overheated to cuts that needed to be stitched to a broken arm and gashed head after a poor guy intently admiring the city fell down a long set of stone steps. They ended up keeping the doors open until seven o'clock when finally the last patients had been treated and were on their way.

With a last swipe of antibacterial wipes along the countertops, she stepped back, satisfied that the exam rooms were ready for the following day. Time to maybe do some evening walking around the city she still had barely toured, then have another wonderful dinner somewhere. Her breath suddenly hitched in her chest as she stood at the sink washing her hands, and she didn't have to turn to know the figure that came to stand close behind her was Enzo. And how did her heart and lungs know work was over and she could think about *him* again, darn it? Being able to concentrate on their patient load all day had convinced her she was over it.

Trying hard to pretend she wasn't ridiculously aware of him, she nonchalantly dried her hands on a towel. Which was tugged from her fingers before a large warm hand grasped hers, the other sliding a cool glass of sparkling water into her palm.

"You've had a long day, and you're probably thirsty. Thanks for hanging in there so long."

"You did, too." She let her eyes meet his over the glass as she took a drink, thinking how very thoughtful he was to have brought it to her. She hadn't even realized she was thirsty—how had he? "And no thanks are needed. That's why I'm here."

"Still, you did a great job. Even not speaking Italian, it amazes me how well you're able to communicate with the locals anyway."

"Hey, I'm learning to speak Italian! A little, anyway. A few words and phrases."

"Yes, you are. Even Venetian Italian." He smiled. "Pretty soon you'll be talking like a native."

"Wouldn't that be wonderful? Sadly, that's probably not a reality, in just a few months." And she'd probably forget all of it after she went back home. Still, the idea of being able to pretend for at least a little while that she was part of this amazing city filled her heart with some emotion she couldn't quite place.

"You never know. I'm impressed with your progress."

"Um…thanks." The admiration in his gaze made her feel warm, or maybe it was his closeness, and she took another big swig of water to cool it before setting the glass on the sink. "I better get going."

"To where?"

She moved to her cupboard to grab her things, hyperaware that he followed. Since she didn't yet have any idea where, and didn't want to think too hard about what *he* might be up to that night, she tried for a joke. A joke she couldn't deny she hoped would needle him a little. "Maybe I have a date."

Even from the corner of her eye, she could see him stop dead. "A date?"

"You know, where you eat somewhere with someone, and explore a bit? A date."

"With who?"

She turned to him and folded her arms across her chest, absurdly pleased that she'd gotten the surprised and disconcerted expression from him she'd wanted. "What's with the questions? You got out of me all I know about Shay, and, since you accomplished that on *our* date, what I do outside the clinic isn't really your business, is it? Maybe me going on a date would finally prove to you that I'm not here because I was pursuing you or something."

"First, you knew when we met that I wanted to learn more about the woman my brother was to marry. Second, I've apologized for the things I said. I realize how stupid it was of me, now that I've gotten to know you better and see the kind of person you are. I'm truly sorry it even crossed my mind to accuse you of that. But there probably is one thing you don't know that you should." The small hallway felt even smaller as he moved close. "Which is that being with you that night was the best thing that's happened to me in a long time."

For once, the eyes meeting hers weren't laughing, or suspicious. His brows weren't dipped into a frown. His lips weren't curved into a teasing smile. Instead, his expression was serious and sincere and her heart started beating in double time. She tried to shore up her defenses because the last thing she needed was the complication of a man who hadn't tried to get in touch with her after their oh-so-memorable night together, who'd been suspicious of her when she'd first come back to Venice, and who was her boss to boot.

And never mind that it was a beyond tempting complication that seemed more tempting with every second that passed.

"I've got to go." She turned and hurriedly grabbed her stuff, shut the cupboard door, and started to move past him, but his hand reached for her arm to stop her. Slid slowly down her skin to twine his warm fingers with hers.

"A long day deserves a nice night," he said quietly. "For both of us. Would you join me for dinner? Then a little more touring of Venice to see things we didn't see last time? Unless you must honor your date, of course."

"I… I think it can be rescheduled." She couldn't help that her response sounded a little breathy, because the way he was looking at her and touching her seemed to steal every molecule of oxygen from her lungs. Making her feel the same way she'd felt two months ago that first night they'd met.

"*Bene.* You have a change of clothes here? I think you'll like what I have in mind."

CHAPTER SIX

"I'm PRETTY SURE that was the best dinner I've ever had. Though I fear I may gain ten pounds by the time I leave here." Aubrey sat back in her chair and watched Enzo pay the bill, his head tipped downward as he did. The night lights by the canal touched the silky black hair that he wore slightly long, and she couldn't help but admire the adorable little waves curling against his neck that were usually a bit hidden by his lab coat. When he looked back up at her with the smile that had dazzled her two months ago and again tonight, her silly heart skipped a beat.

The evening with him had been wonderful, as she'd known it would be. Magical, just like the first night she'd met him. Getting to roam romantic and incredible Venice, not just once, but twice with a man as amusing, intelligent, and physically beautiful as Enzo Affini was something she'd never forget.

Hadn't forgotten even a little in her two months away from Venice.

No wonder she'd fallen into bed with him last time. Not that she had any intention of repeating that all too memorable experience, especially knowing now that he wasn't really perfect in every way.

"Between seeing patients and touring the city, we've walked a lot today. You needed the sustenance." Enzo stood, and why did just his smile keep making her feel a little weak in the knees? His hand wrapped around hers as it had on and off all evening, and it felt perfect and electric and she wasn't sure how much of that was the magic of Venice, and how much was the magic of Enzo Affini. A very lethal combination. "Let's take the *vaporetto* to my boat, hmm? Then I will take you to your house."

Boat? Her tummy tightened at the suggestion— as much as she adored Venice, being on the water made her nervous—and she drew a deep breath to calm it. "You mean your house."

"It's not my house again yet. Unless you mean you want to go back to the house I'm living in, instead?"

His eyebrows were raised, and his dark eyes shone with both amusement and the banked-down heat she'd seen in them on and off all day.

"No way. I could be a stalker, remember? Not smart of you to take a chance. And we work together now. But I appreciate your asking for clarification," she said in a prim voice that got a chuckle out of him.

They headed toward the water taxi, and the closer they got, the more her breath quickened until she felt she might hyperventilate.

Stop being stupid. Being around water all the time while you're here is going to help you get over this, right?

Still, staring at the dark sky surrounded by even darker water as they stepped onto the taxi, she found herself gritting her teeth and hanging tightly on to his arm. She was glad it was far less crowded than earlier that night, which had just added to her anxiety somehow. Despite having plenty of room, he slid his arms around her waist and pulled her back against him just as he had when there had been a few dozen people pressing shoulder to shoulder. The way he held her made her feel safer, ridiculously, and even as she reminded herself again how silly her fears were she found herself clutching the forearms looped across her stomach.

"You don't have to hold me this close anymore, you know." She'd said it to force herself to be brave, but she was more than glad when the arms around her didn't loosen. Her words had come out a little breathy, but she couldn't help that. Between his closeness and her worry, she was surprised she could breathe at all. "I can stand up on a moving boat quite well when people aren't jostling me."

"I know. Which should tell you that's not why I'm holding you close." His voice was soft, his lips right next to her ear in a feather touch against the shell before moving slowly down to rest below the lobe.

For a split second she was surprised. Until the feel of his mouth on her skin had her relaxing, melting back against him at the deliciousness of it and making her forget that they were on dark water that might swallow her up. That he was her boss and all the other reasons she shouldn't let him kiss her again.

Her head tipped back against his collarbone as her hands caressed the large, warm ones pressing against her belly. It wasn't a conscious invitation for him to explore further, but he obviously read it that way, since she could feel his lips smile against her skin before his mouth moved down her throat, the tip of his tongue touching the base.

"It's a good thing the stop near my boat is close by," he said. "Otherwise I might have to kiss you right here in front of everyone. Not that Venetians would mind, but tourists, maybe yes."

"I thought kissing wasn't allowed between clinic employees."

"It's not. But for just this moment, I want to pretend we don't work together."

"But we do work together." And why had she said that, when only negative things could come of it? Those things being that he'd make her stop working at the clinic after all, or he'd decide not to kiss her. And she definitely wanted both of those things a whole lot whether she should or not.

"Sorry, I can't hear you. The wind's in my ears." With his warm, slightly rough cheek touching her temple, they rode across the water without another word passing between them as the breeze caressed her. It felt wonderful, but not nearly as wonderful as the feel of his skin against hers and the exquisite sensory overload that completely overpowered the fear that had squeezed her chest just moments ago.

The *vaporetto* finally docked, and Enzo released her for just a second before grasping her hand to help her off. That familiar fear skittered down her spine again, and she was beyond glad to be off the darn boat. Also glad Enzo had found a very nice way to distract her, and sure hoped she didn't freak out riding on his small boat.

"My skiff is just over there." The pace he kept was so fast, she might have tripped if she hadn't been in the comfy, crepe-soled sandals that were her favorite for long tourist walks.

"Do you have a curfew or something?" she asked breathlessly, feeling nearly dragged behind him as he held her hand tight. "Do you turn into a pumpkin at midnight? Oh, wait, that was Cinderella's coach, not the Prince."

He turned his head to flash a grin at her that somehow managed to look impish and sexily seductive at the same time. "Guess you'll have to stay with me until midnight to find out, hmm?"

Then just as he'd practically started sprinting the second they got off the boat, he came to such an abrupt stop in the shadows beyond a streetlamp, she collided into him as he turned toward her.

"Gee, give a girl a warning, would you?" She pressed her free hand to his chest to separate them and found hard muscle there, and heat, and…and…what had she been about to say?

"Sorry. Here's your warning. I'm going to kiss you now."

And with that promise rumbling deeply from his throat, he pulled her flush against that warm, firm chest, lowered his head to hers, and did exactly that.

The kiss started out gentle, sweet, his mouth moving on hers in an unhurried exploration that stole her breath and sent her heart into slow, rhythmic thuds against her ribs. He tasted a little of the Chianti they'd shared, and of fantasies come to life again, and of him.

Especially him.

The hands she had pressed flat against his pectorals slipped upward of their own will to wrap around the back of his neck, and she could feel his palms splay wide on her back as his arms tightened around her. The kiss deepened, their tongues danced, and Aubrey hung on for dear life as her knees weakened under the sweet assault that felt so beyond a mere kiss there wasn't a name for it.

His lips separated from hers, just enough to let her drag in a much-needed breath at the same time his chest heaved against hers. "You taste amazing, *mia bellezza*. Just like you did the last time we were together."

"You...you do, too." And wow, was that ever true. She stared up into his eyes, and even through the darkness she could see the blaze in their deep brown depths. That taste filled her with a hunger she'd felt only one time before, which had been the last time they'd kissed. A hunger for the life adventures she'd promised herself, for moving on from betrayal, for...for Enzo Affini, smart or not.

"I have to tell you something," he said.

The blaze in his eyes was suddenly joined by an odd seriousness. Maybe even troubled, and her chest felt as if it caved in a little. "Oh. You're... you're involved with someone else?"

"No."

"Okay, that's good." More than good, but then that left lots of other possibilities of something even worse. "You still think I'm a stalker? You murder unsuspecting tourist employees and throw them to the sharks?"

"No. Didn't I already tell you I knew I'd been stupid?" His lips curved slightly. "And I don't believe I've ever seen a shark in the lagoon, or one of the canals. But the truth is almost as bad. The Affini men are a bad bet. I hope Shay knows that. And I want you to know it, too."

"Why?" She searched his face, wondering why he'd gone from kissing her breathless to pulling back like this. And should she really be worried about her friend? "In what way are you a bad bet?"

"Just take my word for it." His expression was downright grim now, even as his eyes still looked at her as if kissing her again was as high on his list of desires as it was on hers, and his hands held her waist so tightly she expected to be pulled back against that hard chest at any moment.

"Shay's a big girl. She's planning on her relationship with your brother to be temporary, and what's best for the baby," she said. "As for me,

I'm a big girl, too. I'm not betting on you. I'm just enjoying kissing you. A lot. And I don't think kissing and…and stuff has anything to do with betting. Does it? You're completely confusing me here."

"Aubrey." He said her name in a low voice that held a smile and something else that made every inch of her insides vibrate, and she found herself moving against him instead of waiting for him to draw her closer. "I know you can't be confused about how much I enjoy kissing you. Even though I shouldn't. And if you are, I'll have to make it clearer."

And with that, he lowered his mouth to hers. Kissed her until all thoughts and questions disappeared, replaced by heat and want and a desire so intense, she felt woozy from it. After long, breathless minutes, he raised his head, lifting one warm hand to cup her cheek, running his thumb across her moist lower lip.

"Are you sure you don't want to quit working at the clinic and just have a hot affair with me instead?"

"Not fair to ask me that question right after you've kissed me like that." And was that ever true. The way her insides were quivering told her to hand in her notice that very second. Who needed work when she could have Enzo Affini for a few months? "But, no, much as I'm tempted, working at the clinic is important to me."

"I know." He smiled and slowly pressed his lips to first one cheek, then the other before lightly kissing her mouth. "I was kidding. Sort of."

He released her and stepped back, and she instantly missed his warmth. "I should get home now. To your home. I mean, your home that's temporarily my home." Lord, kissing the man had clearly shaken her brain as much as the rest of her.

"Thanks for making that clear." Enzo's impish smile was back in full force, and he reached for her hand. "Tomorrow when we see one another at work, we'll pretend tonight didn't happen. If we can."

"Yes. I'm sure I can manage that." Which was a total lie. Her still-tingling lips and wobbly knees told her that, for her at least, pretending that would be impossible.

For the first time all day, there was a lull in the action at the clinic, and Aubrey took the opportunity to get a cold drink and catch her breath, glad the office was about to close. Crazy busy days there had left her with little time to think about the evening she'd spent exploring the city with Enzo. To think about how it had felt when he'd held her and kissed her, which was a very good thing.

During clinic hours, there hadn't been more than a few quick moments to reflect on their odd and confusing relationship. Learning they worked well together, and were able to set aside their attraction to one another while taking care of patients, was a relief. But the other times? When there were gaps between patients? The heat they kept on a back burner would suddenly flare into a warm simmer in an instant.

A teasing grin, or a gentle finger flick to her cheek, or a long look from his dark eyes, would tell her he was remembering their kisses, or maybe even thinking about that first night they'd met over two months ago. Then she'd recall exactly how all that had felt, which would leave her a little short of breath.

So, what were they going to do about it? Was Enzo going to stick to the "keep their distance" thing? Did she want to? And really, hadn't they already violated that rule at least a little?

She had no idea what the answers were, but maybe trying to make a few friends in Venice would keep her from thinking about him so much when they weren't working together. Meet some of the UWWHA nurses who worked at the hospital, or get involved with the various restoration and preservation groups and learn more about the city and its history and challenges.

Yes. That would be a good plan. Learn something, maybe contribute as well, and have more things on her mind than Enzo Affini.

Aubrey was just about to pull out her tablet to see about any meetings the organizations might have scheduled, and look at the UWWHA social loop to see if any of the nurses might be planning a get-together that night, when Nora came into the back hallway.

"We have a Russian couple here. Wife is twenty-five weeks pregnant and is feeling uncomfortable. I'm going to bring her to exam room two."

"All right." Aubrey washed her hands, then greeted the couple with a smile. "Hello. Tell me why you're here."

"My wife is pregnant. Not feeling okay." The man's expression was strained, and his English was hard to understand. Aubrey knew difficulty communicating usually made patients feel even more anxious, and she smiled wider to try to reassure him.

"Tell me how you're not feeling okay," she said to the dark-haired woman, who looked to be in her thirties and reminded Aubrey a little of their Russian housekeeper, Yana, who'd ruled the roost for years when she'd been growing up. "Are you in pain?" Aubrey repeated the word in Russian, hoping to gain her confidence. She didn't speak much of the language, but could manage the basics.

"No." The woman looked at her with surprise, then a smile as she cupped her hands around her round belly, speaking rapidly in Russian until Aubrey had to stop her.

"I'm sorry, I don't understand. I only know a few words, from an old friend."

The woman stopped speaking, but still smiled. "Okay. Just, um, balling. Here."

"Cramping?"

"Yes." She nodded and seemed a little relieved that Aubrey understood what she was trying to say. "Cramping."

"All right. Let's put a gown on you, then get your feet up, and I'll take a listen to baby." She helped the woman undress, then had her lie down on the exam table. After putting a few pillows beneath her legs, she pressed a stethoscope to the woman's belly, relieved to hear a steady heartbeat there. "Baby's heartbeat is normal, so that's good. I'm going to talk to the doctor, okay? Be right back." She patted the woman's shoulder, adjusted the pillows, then went to look for Enzo.

His office door was open, and she was glad to find him there filling out paperwork. "We have a patient who's twenty-five weeks pregnant and experiencing cramping. Baby's heartbeat is steady. Do you want me to do an ultrasound? Or do you want to do an internal exam first?"

He looked up and her heart gave an unfortunate little kick when his dark eyes met hers. Hadn't she just been feeling proud that the simmer between them was mostly absent when they were working? "I'll come do the exam, then we'll decide."

Enzo gave the couple his usual, calm smile, asked questions about how she was feeling, explained what he was going to do, then snapped on gloves as Aubrey helped adjust the patient's position. "You'll feel me touching you, and some pressure, okay? This will just take a moment."

Aubrey watched Enzo's face as he examined the woman's cervix, and though his expression didn't change she could tell instantly that he didn't like what he'd found.

He took off his gloves as Aubrey moved their patient into a more modest position, keeping her legs elevated on the pillows. "I'm afraid there is some dilation of the cervix. Not much, but more than should be there at twenty-five weeks. I want you to go to the hospital for treatment that we can't give you here."

"Hospital? No." The woman suddenly looked a little mulish. "We are on vacation. No hospital."

Enzo glanced at Aubrey, and his look told her loud and clear that he might need backup about this. "If you go into preterm labor, your baby could be born way too soon. It's important that you have the baby monitored for a bit. If they determine that baby is trying to come too early, there are medications that can be given to you through an IV that will stop the process and let baby grow inside you longer. Depending on what they find, they may even want to give you steroid injections to be sure baby's lungs will develop before it's born."

"We go home soon. I will see the doctor there."

The husband hadn't said a word, and it seemed clear that he'd go along with whatever his wife wanted.

"Please let me call the hospital. An extra day or two here is worth your baby being born healthy, isn't it?"

"No. Thank you."

The woman swung her legs over the table and picked up her clothes, clearly intent on leaving. Enzo opened his mouth to say something more, but Aubrey put her hand on his arm to stop him. Her Russian might not be very good, but she understood this woman a little and wanted to give it a try.

A halting conversation with the patient finally had her yielding, and her expression went from stubborn to resigned. Enzo's eyebrows were raised, but he didn't say another word except to tell Aubrey he'd call for the ambulance boat to take the woman to the hospital, probably worried that he'd jinx the process and she'd change her mind.

By the time the ambulance came the office was closed for the day, and it was all Aubrey could do not to drop into a chair and stay there awhile. Enzo returned through the back door after talking with the EMTs, raising his eyebrows at her.

"When were you going to tell me you had special skills with difficult patients? That was amazing."

"I just got lucky." She had to admit she felt good the situation had gone well. Glad the woman and her baby were going to get the help they needed. "Our Russian housekeeper, Yana, was the most stubborn woman I've ever known. She was very suspicious of doctors and hospitals, and refused to see anyone but a Russian doctor whose practice was almost a hundred miles from our town. I channeled my memories of why she felt the way she did when I was talking to our patient. I guess it worked."

"I guess it did." He reached for her hand and brought it to his lips, his eyes smiling at her above it. Heating, too, as that *thing* that was always simmering there between them started to boil a little higher. "You are a constant surprise, Aubrey Henderson."

"I try to keep you guessing and on your toes, Dr. Affini," she said lightly, hoping he couldn't tell that just the touch of his lips on her hand and the way he was looking at her had her heart doing a little tap dance.

"You successfully do that every day. In more ways than one."

The dark eyes meeting hers were full of admiration, maybe a little confusion, and a whole lot of desire. She recognized it, because she could feel it melting her bones.

"Aubrey."

His deep voice vibrated through her, and her answer back was breathless. "Yes?"

"Would you join me for a cruise on the water to see some of the islands in the northern lagoon? They're very different from the glamorous Venice you've seen, and one has interesting buildings and church ruins I believe you'd enjoy. I'll pick up some things for a picnic dinner. What do you say?"

He was watching her with the small smile touching his lips that was always so appealing, but the question in his eyes seemed to say that what he was asking was important to him. And how could she say no to an excursion to a part of the lagoon she might not get to see her entire time here, if not for him? The thought of cruising on that dark water made her stomach squeeze, but she knew if there was one person who could make her face her fear of that, it was this caring and empathetic man.

"I'd love to. But I'm happy to get the food together."

"Let me. I have favorite delis I know that will pack us a picnic you won't forget. I'll pick you up at the house at six, *sì*?"

"*Sì.*" Her chest bubbled with pleasure just at the thought of spending another evening with Enzo Affini, even as she promised herself it absolutely would not end anything like the first delicious one they'd shared.

CHAPTER SEVEN

WITH BAGS OF food and a few bottles of wine from one of the family wineries at his feet, Enzo sent his boat through the canal toward his old home. He hadn't looked forward to an evening with a woman this much in a long time. Not since the recent night they'd spent touring and eating and kissing. Not since the incredible night he'd spent with Aubrey two months ago, and he didn't have to think too hard about what all that meant.

Maybe this was a bad idea. Maybe it wasn't. Maybe it didn't matter either way, because he'd given up on keeping their relationship strictly business, not just because he'd failed miserably at it. Because he'd come to believe that, unbelievably coincidental as it had seemed that Aubrey had shown up in his life, there'd been a reason for it. And not the reason he'd originally wondered.

It was meant to be that he and Aubrey would have four amazing months to spend time together. For her to have a native Venetian show her the most amazing city in the world. For him to have something in his life to enjoy while he dealt with the very stressful and unenjoyable battle to get his mother's house back from the brink of destruction, and into the family fold again.

The more he was around Aubrey, the more he wanted her. Warm and smart and a little sassy, and how was he to resist that lethal combination?

Clearly, the answer was that he couldn't. And he'd given up trying.

His heart gave a strange little kick in his chest when he saw Aubrey waiting for him next to the dock. She smiled and waved, and he nearly ran the boat into one of the wooden posts, he was so intent on looking at her beautiful face and body, her silky hair lifting a little in the breeze.

He managed to safely secure the boat right next to her. A gust of wind blew her dress up a little, and was it his fault that he was below her and had to look?

"Hey!" Both her hands pressed down her skirt and she frowned at him. "No peeking up my dress."

"Need I point out that I've already had the pleasure of seeing way more of you than that?"

She gasped, but it almost sounded like a shocked laugh, so he was pretty sure her offense was mock. Though why he'd let such a thing fall out of his mouth, he wasn't sure. Or maybe he was, because he couldn't help that the vision of her beautiful, naked body often filled his mind.

"That kind of remark definitely doesn't qualify for us having that professional, friendly relationship we're trying to have."

"That was friendly, wasn't it?"

"Maybe in Italy. At home it's called sexual harassment."

"Is it? To me, sexual harassment is more like—"

"Stop now, before I call the UWWHA on you. And refuse to come on this excursion after all."

He'd already told himself to shut up already and laughed at how outraged she somehow managed to look, even when her beautiful eyes were twinkling. "Sorry. I'll behave. Come on. Your chariot awaits."

"Does Prince Affini say that to all the girls he picks up?"

"Only the ones he wants to picnic with." He reached for her hand. "Watch your step."

She hesitated for a moment before finally extending her hand. He folded her soft palm in his, surprised at the strength of her grip as she stepped carefully into the boat. So carefully, in fact, he looked up at her instead of at her sexily sandaled feet, suddenly realizing she looked surprisingly scared. "Does getting into the boat worry you?"

"Of course not. Um…okay, yes. I'd hoped I'd be so brave you wouldn't notice."

Her teeth sank into that delectably full lower lip of hers, and he let go of the post to grasp her elbow, keeping her steady on the gently bobbing boat as he lowered her onto the seat. "What should I have noticed?" But he had a feeling he already knew.

Wide blue-gray eyes met his, filled with embarrassment and worry. "I'm… I'm afraid of water. Like, dark lake water or ocean water. It's silly, I know. Ridiculous. I can even swim fine and have no problem in a clear swimming pool. But when I was really little, I fell off the dock of the big pond on our property and thought I was going to drown for sure until one of our groundskeepers jumped in and fished me out. I've been weirded out by it ever since."

He hadn't asked about her background, but if they had housekeepers and groundskeepers, that usually meant wealth. But, of course, he'd figured she must be well-to-do when he'd first learned about her donation to restore that fresco.

He remembered the way she'd clung to him on the *vaporetto*, realizing now that perhaps it had been as much about her fear as about wanting to be close to him. Had he not noticed because all he'd been able to think about that night was how much he wanted to kiss and touch her? The alarm in her eyes was more than real, and he thrashed himself for not seeing it before.

"I'm sorry I didn't realize you were scared.

I wish you'd told me before now." He sat close enough to wrap his arm around her, this time to comfort instead of maneuvering into a good position to kiss her, though he couldn't help but think about that, too. "Perhaps driving around on the canals and riding more often in the *vaporetto* will help you manage it better, hmm? Though I have to say I'm surprised at your insistence on staying in Venice instead of going to the mainland. A woman with a fear of water clearly likes to torture herself if she wants to live in a city built on water."

He smiled at her, relieved to see her smile back, even if it was a weak effort. "Actually, I did it on purpose. Not to torture myself, but to deal with it. Get past it. My mother had a terrible fear of being in public places around a lot of people, and it was paralyzing for her. I promised myself I wouldn't live my life like that, that I'd figure out a way to get over it. Four months here should do the trick, don't you think?"

"When did your mother pass?" he asked quietly, understanding well that pain and loss.

"Just over a year ago." She looked away across the water, and the pain on her face was so intense, he squeezed her shoulder in support. When she turned back to him, her smile was wider, but still forced. A clear message that they were closing the subject. "I'm starving and very excited about this picnic idea. Where are we going again?"

"To an island in the northern lagoon that's mostly deserted, but beautiful in its own way. The marshes and mud flats around it are totally different from here, and much of the island itself is marshy with rough fields. It's quiet, unlike the busyness of Venice. I think you'll like it. And, Aubrey?"

"What?"

"I promise I won't let you fall overboard."

She smiled, but it didn't banish the worry in her eyes, and his mouth lowered to hers for a soft kiss to reassure her before he'd even realized he'd done it. And that simple touch of his lips to hers made him want so much more.

When his lips parted from hers, he was glad

he'd kissed her, because the eyes wide on his were filled with something very different from worry now, and it was all he could do not to go back for another, deeper kiss.

He drew in a breath and forced himself to stand again, his arm around her waist as he moved them to the rear seat.

"Sit in the back with me. It'll make the bow sit a little high in the water, but you'll be close to me." Normally he would have had her stay in the center of the boat for better weight distribution, but he wanted to keep his arm around her. Make her feel secure. And it had nothing to do with wanting to touch her soft skin and hold her close. And he was getting really good at kidding himself when it came to Aubrey Henderson.

They passed boats like his, larger tour boats, and the ferry that stopped at a few of the islands. Her excited exclamations at the various sights made him smile, glad he'd had the idea to bring her here. He watched her point at old buildings and churches as they went by, and each time she did she'd turn to look at him with a bright smile.

He stared into her eyes as she talked, wondering how she described their color. Sometimes they were the gray of the water, tinted with a blue reflection of the sky. Other times they seemed more blue than gray, with interesting flecks of green and gold. Holding a smile inside that she was able to enjoy the ride in spite of her fear, he felt as buoyant as the boat skimming across the water.

"So, where exactly does Dante live? And, I guess Shay now, too."

Her odd tone of voice had him stealing another look at her. She wore a slight frown, and her lips were cutely twisted as though she was wondering about that marriage as he was, which lightened Enzo's heart even more. If she wasn't too sure about the two of them marrying, that would mean there was no agenda on Shay's part, just a situation where a night of lovemaking had led to unexpected consequences.

"Dante's home is on the Lido di Venezia. The very long island you can see past Guidecca, which is across from San Marco's."

"Is it as old as yours? I mean, the house I'm living in now?"

"No. His is practically new. Built in the fifteen-hundreds. Needs a bit of work, though."

She laughed. "Only in Italy is something built in the fifteen-hundreds practically new."

"Much of the rest of Europe would object to that statement. Though I believe our history is the most interesting, which isn't bias, of course."

"It is. It's incredible. Imagine knowing who your ancestors were so long ago, and that they lived and loved in the very house you grew up in. You have to get that house back, no matter what."

The fierceness on her face reflected just how his heart and gut felt on the matter, and it amazed him that she seemed to understand that. "I agree, *bellezza*. Believe me. And I will, no matter what it takes."

He didn't want to think about all that now, and the tough odds against him. He wanted to enjoy a special evening with this very special woman.

They sat in silence as they approached the island, and he didn't try to analyze the sense of peace he felt being with her at the same time he felt utterly wired. "I'm going to dock here. We'll walk along the canal, but, unlike the ones you've seen before, this one will be practically deserted. Then I'll show you the old churches, and then we'll have our picnic on a favorite green space Dante and I used to bring girls."

"I can imagine what you both had planned when you did that."

"And sometimes those plans would backfire if the mosquitoes came out. Smelly repellent isn't quite as appealing as cologne."

"Except rubbing it on the girls would have been a good excuse to touch them."

"There was that, yes."

Her soft laughter slid inside him, and he reached to tuck the silky strands of hair that had escaped her ponytail behind her ear. Let his fingers travel down her jaw before sliding his hand down her arm to hold hers as they exited the boat.

Her exclamations and excitement as they walked along the deserted canal made him feel as if he were seeing everything with new eyes himself, despite having been there dozens of times. They trudged over the grasslands and saw the ancient churches and abandoned homes, and she seemed so pleased, he was glad he'd brought her out here, despite her fear of the water.

"You're right—this place is very different from Venice." Aubrey spread the blanket over the flat, overgrown grass next to the lagoon. "Feels almost wild, you know?"

"Yeah." He wanted to tell her that watching her tempting rear move around as she bent over to straighten the blanket was making him feel a little wild, too. Because hauling her into his arms, lying down on that blanket, and kissing her until neither of them could breathe seemed like a much better idea than a picnic. He inhaled a deep breath of the salty air and concentrated on pulling out the food. "After we eat, we'll take the boat to meander through the channels a little more, where we'll probably see wildlife, then we'll head back."

The picnic food seemed to taste even better than usual, and he was glad he'd brought one of their wineries' best vintages to share with her. "Did Shay tell you about the Affini estates in Tuscany? We have extensive vineyards, and several wineries. Dante and I are pretty happy with this batch of Chianti. I hope you like it."

"It's really good." Her eyes closed briefly as she took a sip, apparently letting it linger in her mouth. The expression on her face reminded him of the night they'd made love, and he turned his attention to the horizon to subdue the way his body reacted to the memories. "And believe it or not, Shay and I really haven't had a chance to talk about more than the, um, situation. I don't really know much about the Affini family other than what you've shared with me."

"And that's probably just as well." Talking about his family situation was one sure way to kill his libido, and he managed to get them settled onto the blanket without laying her down on it and kissing her breathless.

As they ate they shared stories of patients that had both of them laughing, along with a few that brought tears to Aubrey's eyes, turning them into another fascinating shade of gray-blue tinted with green.

"What color are your eyes?"

She paused from eating a chunk of bread and looked up in surprise. "My eyes?"

"Yes. I'm slightly color blind, and every time I look at them, I wonder."

"That must be so strange! Do you have to spend your life figuring out what color things are, or are you just used to not being sure?"

"Neither. Most of the time I don't particularly care." He leaned closer, lifted his hands to cup the softness of her cheeks as he turned her face, watching her pretty eyes catch the lowering sunlight. "But knowing the color of your eyes feels important."

"They're…they're just a mix of colors. Change with what I'm wearing, and the light, and how I'm feeling, I guess. I always wished I could say they were blue or green or gray, but never knew how to answer that on my driver's license questionnaire."

She smiled, but he could feel her pulse fluttering against his fingers, her breath skittering across his face, and knew she felt the electricity strumming the air between them, too.

He lowered his mouth to hers, sipping the Chianti from her lush lower lip before delving deeper, feeling the hot connection zing between them that happened every time their mouths met. Kept kissing her as she slid her arms around his neck and pulled him close. Felt her melting into him, and he lowered her slowly to the blanket before both of them ended up just toppling over.

His hand found its way to the soft skin of her thigh, tracking up inside her skirt, and her gasp into his mouth inflamed him. The only thought in his head was getting her naked and kissing and touching her everywhere and he was making progress on that mission until the sound of voices and laughter somehow made it through the sexual fog in his brain.

He barely managed to break the kiss, lifting his head toward the sounds. Sure enough, not too far down the grassy area, a group of people, likely tourists who'd decided to go off the beaten path, had unloaded off a hired boat.

"Well, damn." He dropped another quick kiss to her mouth before he made himself sit up, taking her hand to help her do the same.

"I thought you said this island is practically deserted." Somehow her eyes were laughing a little at the same time they looked as dazed as he felt. Her tongue slipped out to lick her lips, and he nearly groaned, thinking about what they'd been doing just seconds ago and how good it had felt and where it might have been headed next.

"It is. Usually. Just our luck, hmm?"

"Maybe the gods of professional relationships are looking out for us."

That got a laugh out of him. "I hope not. Roman gods can be pretty ruthless. And I don't know about you, but I'm seriously thinking about crossing them."

Golden fingers of light spilled across her shining hair as she let out a low laugh, which had him pulling her close for another soft kiss. Behind her, the sun sank to just above the grasses and murky water, and Enzo let go of her to pick up his wineglass and tip the last of it into his mouth. But the taste of Aubrey still lingered.

"We better get going before it's so dark you can't see a bit of the lagoon life."

"Okay." Her last sip of her own wine was followed by what sounded like a very happy sigh, and she sent him a smile almost as brilliant as the setting sun. "I bet I'll more than like it. This has been wonderful. Thank you for bringing me."

"Thank you for joining me." He helped her back into the boat and couldn't remember a time he'd felt quite this deeply connected with a woman. "I love it out here. Haven't found a good reason to come lately. You're my reason."

"I like being your reason."

Their gazes met and held. Something about the words made them seem more important than they should have. He didn't know exactly why, but the feeling hung between them, sweet and intimate and suspended in the thick lagoon air. Enzo found himself just looking at her as they sat close on the small seat, her hip and arm warm against

his, and it felt about as right as anything he'd
ever felt before.

"I have to ask you something," she said, her
gaze steady on his. "Why didn't you ever call
me when I was in Rome?"

An easy question with a hard answer. "I thought
about it more times than I could count. Had the
phone in my hand ready to dial, but stopped myself. I wasn't sure about Shay and my brother, and
if she had planned what happened. And you were
her friend, which seemed like it could be a problem. Plus I had the issues with the house going
on, and I just… I guess I felt like being with you
was a complication I didn't need."

"And then it just got more complicated."

"Yeah. But somehow that complication seems
more than worth it now." He drew her close for
another long, sweet kiss, until he managed to pull
back to get the boat on its way. The movement
put an inch or two between them, and he instantly
missed the feel of her body touching his.

"Soon I'll be turning off the motor and using

the oars so we can slip quietly through the channel. Parts of it are only two feet deep." Maybe talking about the place would get his mind back on track. Away from her soft skin and lush mouth. "Depending on the flow of the rivers and wash of tides from the Adriatic, if you lean over you'll see fish, crab, squid—all of the many things you can find on restaurant menus in the city."

"It almost reminds me of the fish farming on the coast near my house."

"Venetians like to scoff at talk about the 'new' art of fish farming, since we've been doing it for hundreds of years."

"You Venetians seem to like to scoff a lot at anyone who doesn't have the history you do."

"Which is most everyone, Ms. New World."

They exchanged grins as he cut the motor and let the boat slide into the marshy channel. Aubrey leaned over just a couple inches to peer over the side of the boat, then, as the boat slightly rocked, grabbed his arm so tightly it hurt.

"Ouch," he said, extricating her fingernails

from his skin, holding her arm up against his body instead. "I'm wishing this boat had a mast for you to hold on to instead of my flesh." He dropped a kiss onto her cheek and smiled at her, hoping she'd relax.

"I'm sorry."

"No need to be sorry. But remember what I said? Only two or three feet deep here. If you did fall out, you'd get a mud bath as much as you'd get wet. But you won't fall—the boat is steady, promise. I'm here to steady you, too. Making you feel safe is, right now, my priority in life."

"That's a…a very sweet thing to say. And being scared is so silly, I know." She sat up straighter and looked embarrassed, which made him wish he hadn't teased her. "I'm trying."

"I know. And that impresses me more than you know." He stroked her soft inner arm as he tucked her closer. "Do you have any idea how many people just accept their fears and don't try to do a thing about it? You're already way ahead of every one of them."

"Thank you." Her eyes were wide and troubled

as they clung to his. "I'll get there. I— Oh!" She pointed behind him. "Look at that huge bird! What is it? Is it stuck in the lagoon?"

CHAPTER EIGHT

ENZO TURNED TO see the bird, which had doubtless just dived into the water. "It's a cormorant. They're everywhere out here. The lagoon's bounty of fish and shellfish are a daily buffet."

"It looks trapped or something."

He looked again, then even closer. Was the bird really floundering? "Let's go take a look." With the oar shoved into the mud, he pushed the boat through the marshland.

"You look like a gondolier when you do that. Is that another of your many skills?"

"Is that a real question of a man who grew up here? I look exceptionally good in the striped shirt and beribboned hat."

Her laughter faded as they drifted up close to the bird and it became clear that it truly was in distress. "Is that…? What is that on it? Oil?"

"Don't know. Something like that." He tried to maneuver the boat close enough to see if there was something they could do without making the bird panic, jamming the oar deep into the mud to bring the boat to a stop. "With the industrial plants at Marghera and near the causeway, chemicals from agriculture, and all the tankers and cruise ships that come by, our pollution problems have gotten worse. We've put in buffer strips of trees and shrubs along the edges of the lagoon to try to catch it, but it's not a perfect solution."

"Poor bird!" Aubrey leaned over the edge of the boat toward the bird, obviously forgetting about being afraid of the water. "What can we do?"

"It's not completely covered in the oil, so that's good. Probably just dived into a single gob that had fallen off a ship. It still looks fairly healthy, I think." He glanced at her. Normally, when things like this happened, he'd get the bird on the boat and take it to one of his veterinary friends, but he knew from experience that sometimes the birds didn't like that too well. He didn't want to see Aubrey get splattered with the oil or, worse, pecked and injured, especially when they were on the water, which worried her.

"It won't be healthy for long. You know as well as I do that it won't be able to clean itself enough, or if it does the oil it eats off its feathers will make it sick."

"And how do you know this?"

"Just because you're a doctor and a prince and a native Venetian doesn't mean nobody else knows as much as you, Dr. Affini," she said with great dignity. "I volunteered off the coast of California when there was an oil slick once."

"A woman of many talents." He had to laugh as he said it, even as one or two of those talents that came to mind weren't funny, they were amazing, and he shouldn't be thinking about them. "So you won't freak out if I bring it on board and it flaps around? We'll have to try to secure it with something."

"The blanket will work." While she rummaged through the picnic bag, he got the medical bag he always kept with him in case there was an emergency, and snapped on the gloves.

"If we do this, I can't promise that you won't get covered with oil, or even bitten."

"I can handle both of those things. And I know a certain quack doctor who is very knowledgeable about bird bites and pecks." Her eyes laughed into his. "But we just need to hold him tight, right?"

"Hopefully right. But sometimes things don't always go as planned, you know?" He grinned back. "All right, then. After I put him in it, I'll keep his beak closed while you wrap him and hold him as tight as you can. Tell me when you're ready."

"Ready."

He draped the blanket over her shoulders, then smoothed it down over her legs as much as possible, and was it his fault he had to linger on each of those spots as he did?

"What kind of man uses rescuing a bird as an excuse to fondle a woman?"

"A man who keeps trying not to touch you, but can't help himself."

The seductive look she sent back to him jabbed

him right in the solar plexus, along with a few other notable places, and that thing that kept shimmering between them lit the air. This time it was Aubrey who leaned in for the kiss, and he was only too happy to meet her halfway. Her mouth was sweet and soft and pliant, and if he hadn't had the damn gloves on he would have held her face in his hands, tipped it back, and kissed her until neither of them could think anymore, but that would have to wait.

He pulled back, loving the way her lips stayed parted as she stared at him. "Hold that thought, okay? We have a good deed to do."

Maybe she was having as much trouble talking as he was, because she just nodded. He turned to slowly, carefully reach for the bird, bracing himself in case it tried to fly up into him. When he grasped its body, holding its wings down as firmly as he could, he was glad the bird only wrestled weakly to get away.

"Coming to you on the count of three. One, two, three." He pulled the bird from the water, pressed it into the cloth over Aubrey's waiting arms, then lifted one hand to slide his fingers around the bird's beak as she wrapped it and held it close to her breasts.

Lucky bird.

"I... I think I'm good," she said. Enzo used his free hand to help wrap it, while holding the beak tightly as the bird jerked its head up and down, trying to get loose. He took from his wrist the rubber band that he'd grabbed from his bag earlier and wrapped it around the beak. For having fairly small arms, it looked as if Aubrey had the huge bird held good and tight.

"I'm going to let go now, okay?" He watched carefully, ready to contain it if he had to, but the bird seemed to have given up the argument, and Aubrey's elated eyes met his.

"We did it!"

"Haven't gotten him back yet. So don't count your cormorants before they're hatched. Or something like that." She laughed as he snapped off the oily gloves to get the motor going. "I'm not going to go too fast, so it doesn't get scared."

"And so *I* don't get scared, wimp that I am."

She said it without one bit of fear on her excited face, and Enzo's chest filled with something absurd, like maybe pride in her toughness, as he reached to stroke her soft cheek.

"You? A wimp? Wonderful nurse, fear-facer, and bird-rescuer? You, Aubrey Henderson, are a warrior."

All the way back, she talked to the bird in a soothing voice, and Enzo had to smile at how cute she was. His vet friend, Bartolomeo, met them at the dock, and the handoff proved to be a little awkward. Getting Aubrey out of the boat at the same time she held the bird tight wasn't easy, but finally she was standing on the walkway, able to carefully pass the bird to Bart.

"Is it going to be all right, do you think?" Aubrey asked, her happy expression dimmed with concern now.

"Do not worry, *signorina*," Bart said. "You have brought him in good shape. I have all I need to get it cleaned up and hydrated, and an assistant who enjoys helping with birds in trouble. Come to our office to see it in a few days—with a little luck, I think you'll be pleased."

"I'd like that. Seeing how you do things there would be interesting, too."

"Aubrey has told me about some of her many interests, Bart." Enzo smiled at the excitement on her face, despite the splotches of oil on various parts of her skin and dress. "She's participated in bird rescue in the past."

"Maybe you could come work at my veterinary clinic. We can always use extra hands."

"No way," Enzo said, stepping in fast before she had a chance to think about that. "I need her nursing skills at the clinic more than you need her giving shots to dogs and cats."

"No promises that I won't try to woo her over to my clinic instead, Enzo."

His friend's face might be grinning, but it showed loud and clear that he was attracted to Aubrey, too, and what man in his right mind wouldn't be? The feeling of possessiveness that suddenly filled Enzo's chest was unfamiliar, but there was no denying that emotion was what drove him to reach for her hand. To place a kiss to her forehead in a clear message to Bart as to whom she belonged to.

For the moment, at least.

"I appreciate the offer, but I think nursing humans is my calling at this point. Thank you, though," Aubrey said, and Enzo felt relieved that she didn't scowl at him for answering before she could say a word, but squeezed his hand instead.

"Let me know if you change your mind. And now I'd best get this bird taken care of before he decides to dive back into the lagoon. *Arrivederci.*"

Glad the man and the bird were gone, Enzo was able to focus on just Aubrey again. He ran his fingers across the black smudges on her forehead and jaw, only managing to smear them even more. "You're a bit of a mess. And I am, too. The clinic is close by, so I suggest we go there to shower. Unless you gave away my change of clothes again?"

"Funny." She playfully swatted his arm. "I don't have extra clothes there, though. Maybe you should just take me home so I can clean up there."

"No. Because that would be the end of our evening together, and I'm not ready for that." The truth of his statement had him tugging her against him, not caring that the bits of oil on her skin would find their way to his shirt and pants. "Are you?"

"No," she said softly, and the way she smiled into his eyes and snaked her hands around his neck stole his breath. "I'm not."

He touched his lips to her nose and the places on her face that weren't smeared with oil before kissing her for real, and the heat of her mouth felt so arousing, so right, he had to break the kiss and suck in a deep breath before he stripped her naked right there in public.

"Come on. Let's get that oil off you." He grasped her hand and nearly ran the few blocks it took to get to the clinic. He quickly pushed the code into the keypad outside the back door and practically hauled her inside, not able to stop until they were in the locker room next to the shower.

"I'll go in first," she said in a prim voice totally at odds with the twinkle and heat in her eyes. "I'll let you know when it's your turn, Dr. Affini."

"Uh-uh. This job requires two people." He grabbed towels from the stack on the shelf, then washcloths, too, before reaching for her hem. He had the dress off and over her head in one quick movement, then reached around her to get the bra off, too.

"What kind of job are you referring to?" Her fingers were already working his belt, then the button and zipper, too, shoving his pants down his legs. One second later, she had her hands around the waistband of his boxer shorts, inflaming his obvious desire even further until he nearly groaned. "I think I'm handling this okay solo, don't you?"

"You're doing a fine job, yes," he said, his voice a little hoarse. "But once we've taken care of this part, the next jobs will take both of us."

"Jobs, plural? I might need more instruction on this job you're referring to. You might do it differently in this clinic than we do at home." Those beautiful, mysteriously colored eyes met his, and the heat and humor in them weakened his knees almost as much as the way she was touching him.

He opened the shower door, turned the water on, and finished getting both of them naked as fast as he could. "Pretty universal techniques around the world, I'd think. Except there's not one single thing that's just 'usual' when it comes to you, Aubrey Henderson."

The water spraying his back was still a little cold, so he pulled her in front of him to shield her from it until it warmed. Once he'd gotten a washcloth wet, he slathered it with soap. "Here's the two-person job. You can't see the black stuff smeared on your face, and this oil is tough stuff, so I'll have to wash it for you."

The frustration on her face made him chuckle as he gently washed the spot on her forehead. "If this is strictly medical, with you cleaning me like your friend is cleaning the bird, I might have to kill you."

"You had something else in mind, *bellezza*?" He scrubbed off the spot on her jaw, then slowly moved the washcloth down her throat, across her collarbone, and down to her nipple, following with his lips and tongue.

"Um…no. I can see this is…an excellent way to address the problem." She tipped her head back, and as he licked the water from the hollow of her throat and slid the cloth slowly back and forth across her breasts and down between her thighs, her little gasping breaths and the way she touched and stroked him back nearly sent him to his knees.

Which might not be a bad place to be.

So go there, he did. Kneeling before her, he held her sexy, round bottom in his hands and drew her to his mouth. Kissed and touched the slick sweetness of her center as she tangled her hands in his wet hair and made little sounds and it was so good he didn't notice how much her legs were shaking until she dropped to her knees, too, pushing him back onto his rear as she did.

"That was… I couldn't…" She stopped talking. With her lips parted, she stopped talking. Just stared at him with eyes that were filled with

the same intense want that rushed uncontrolla-
bly through his veins and his mind and his heart.

"I know."

It was good that words weren't necessary any
longer, since neither of them seemed able to say
more than two of them in a row. She reached to
touch him, her hands caressing his cheeks down
to his shoulders as he lifted her to him, pressing her warm, wet breasts against his chest. He
was barely aware of the water pouring over their
heads and bodies. All he could think about was
how she felt against him as she positioned herself and eased onto him. All he could see was
how incredible she looked as she moved on him,
needing to touch every part of her he could reach
as she did. Her breasts, her hips. Her thighs and
waist and where they were intimately joined. Her
soft cheeks as he brought her mouth to his for
a deep kiss that seemed to shake his very soul
even as their orgasms shook their bodies. And
when she pressed her torso to his, resting her
face against his throat as their chests rose and
fell in unison, he knew with certainty that he'd

never before experienced anything like the physical pleasure and emotional closeness and mental connection all layered together that he felt at that moment with Aubrey in his arms.

Which was incredible and confusing and scary as hell.

CHAPTER NINE

AUBREY BLINKED AT the orange-yellow early-morning sunlight that spilled through the huge windows of Enzo's childhood home and across the thick cotton comforter. She turned her head and focused her bleary eyes on the oh-so-close chiseled features of Enzo, his head propped up on one hand and his sculpted lips curved in a smile.

"Buongiorno, mia bellezza," he murmured.

He pressed a soft kiss to her forehead, then lazily began twining a strand of her hair through his fingers. His slumberous dark brown eyes were looking at her in a way that told her he was ready to take up where they'd left off last night, and how that could be she had no clue, since three times in one night had been more incredible sex than she'd ever enjoyed in her life.

Than she ever expected to enjoy as much again.

"How can you be so wide-awake? We were up half the night." She rolled slightly toward him because she wanted to feel the warmth of his skin again. Wanted to feel the thud of his heart against her hands as she pressed them to that wide, well-defined chest. Wanted to slip her arms around his strong body and stay held close in his arms for the rest of the day.

For the rest of the time she'd be in Venice, and suddenly a few months didn't feel nearly long enough.

"Sleeping seems like a waste of time when I'm with you."

Oh. Well. When he put it that way, she'd have to agree. "Except sleep is kind of a necessity when we have to be at work in an hour. Or at least I do. Are you working today, too?" It suddenly struck her that Enzo might have scheduled her to work with the other clinic doctor—the one she hadn't even met yet—since their plans to keep that professional distance had gone up in smoke, then seriously hot flames, last night.

"You think I'd have you work with Antonio instead of me? No way. Women fall all over him, and he takes advantage of that. You're stuck working with me instead, Nurse Aubrey, for better or for worse."

She sat up. Did he mean that the way it had sounded? "So what you're saying is you think I'd sleep with any handsome man? Just because I slept with you that first night we met, I want you to know—"

"No, feisty one." He effectively stopped her by pressing his mouth to hers before propping his head on his hand again. He tugged at the strand of hair in his fingers, and the way he grinned in response seemed to show he was enjoying her annoyance. "I'm saying that I don't trust him to not come on to you, then I'd have to beat him up, and the clinic would be down to one doctor. Not the best thing for our many patients, do you think?"

She sank back into the mattress and snuggled up against him, liking his words more than she should. Since when had she ever been attracted to a possessive man?

Apparently, when that man was fun, smart,

delectable Enzo Affini. And since they'd now moved way beyond a simple hookup, she wanted to learn more about him.

"That first night we met," she started to say, "you—"

"Couldn't resist kissing you."

"And prying for information about Shay. Which I told you I know is why you went out with me at all."

"Ah, you're wrong about that. I did want to find out more about the woman my brother was going to marry, but that was most definitely not the only reason I went out with you." Heat emanated from his body as he tugged her closer, and as he nuzzled her neck it was very apparent that he was ready for round four. "The second I spied you from across the room, I was extremely attracted, which alarmed me greatly."

"Alarmed you?"

"Because I thought you were Shay. Remember I told you I'm slightly color blind? Dante had told me she was wearing a green dress, and I thought yours was green." She could tell that the lips traveling across her throat and down to her collarbone were smiling. "Very bad form to lust after your future sister-in-law."

She started to laugh, then squeaked when his mouth found her breast. "I'm trying to have a conversation with you here." He didn't seem to listen, as he moved his attention lower to start nipping at her ribs, but maybe that had something to do with the fact that she was clutching the back of his head and holding him close.

"Converse away." His tongue slipped back up across her nipple and she gasped with the goodness of it before she managed to speak again.

"Tell me why you say you and your brother are bad bets."

She hadn't necessarily wanted to stop his very exciting ministrations, but her question had him lifting his head to look at her, all playfulness gone from his face.

"Because we are."

"People aren't just born bad bets, Enzo."

"And you would be wrong about that." His heavy sigh slid across her skin as he rolled to his back, bringing her with him. He just looked at her, seeming to think awhile before he finally spoke. "The Affini men are afflicted with a bad personality trait. My father's father was notorious for the number of women he kept, with my grandmother pretending to look the other way. My father was even worse, but my mother didn't pretend it wasn't happening. She spent their whole married life trying to change him."

"Did they fight?"

"I'm not sure you could call it that." He turned his head to look at her, and his dark eyes were filled with a peculiar mix of pain and anger and disgust. "My mother would cry and beg for him to stop and love only her, and he would respond that he knew she loved him enough for both of them. I never understood why, but that appeared to be the truth."

"That's…that's terrible! Why did she stay with him? Because of you and Dante?" Aubrey just couldn't imagine having the man she loved constantly cheating. She looked at Enzo as he held her naked body close to his, and realized that if she found out he'd been with another woman while they were sleeping together, it would tear her up inside. That they'd been together only once over two months ago, and a matter of days since then, wouldn't change that. Being together for years? Having children together? Impossible to imagine.

"No." He stroked his finger down her cheek. "We wanted her to leave him. My mother was a happy, loving, joy-filled woman except for this one, terribly painful thing in her life. We knew our home would be a more cheerful place, a better place, if he was out of the house. But even on the day she died, as he stood by her bedside, she told him how much she loved him."

"He must have felt terrible then. Must have told her how much he loved her, too."

A bitter laugh left Enzo's throat. "No. The only person my father loves is himself."

Her throat clogged for the poor woman who had loved a man who hadn't loved her back the same way. For the sons who'd grown up with a cold, selfish man for a father, doubtless feeling confused and hurt about all of it. Thought about her own mother. She'd never spoken of Aubrey's father, which had left Aubrey's imagination to create a larger-than-life dad.

Had her mother loved him? Had he left her? Was that why she'd done what she'd done?"

"And so you see why we are bad bets." He brought her mouth to his for a kiss so sweet, it was hard to imagine that he truly believed that about himself.

"Just because your dad isn't a good person doesn't mean you're not. You know that."

His answer was to kiss her again. "Your turn," he said, tucking her close and playing with her hair some more. "Tell me about your family."

She didn't really want to talk about it. But he'd answered her questions, hadn't he? Fair was fair.

"My mother was a very special person. So smart, and a wonderful, loving mom. We did everything together, until she got sick with cancer." She closed her eyes against the tears that threatened, but he turned her face to make her look into his warm and sympathetic eyes.

"Aubrey. It's okay to cry. I cried when I lost my mother, too. Sometimes I still do, when I think about losing the house she loved. So tell me about the wonderful woman who created such a special daughter."

She swallowed and forced herself to go on. "I told you she was afraid of crowds, of being around more than a few people. But in small groups, she was such an amazing leader. Her passion for the history of our city in Massachusetts, for our home and the other historic homes there, led her to start a number of architectural boards, and to get laws passed that would keep that history, that heritage, from being torn down or irreparably changed."

"We would have gotten along well, your mother and I."

"Yes." That thought managed to make her smile. "You would have."

"And your father?"

That, she definitely didn't want to talk about. "Let's just say he and your father have a lot in common."

"He cheated on her?" His voice had gone low and hard.

"No. Or at least, I have no idea about that. I never knew him until after she died. Other than telling me she got pregnant accidentally when she was only nineteen, she never talked about him. So, growing up, I created who he might be in my mind. Strong and handsome and fun. Someone everybody adored. My imaginary dad loved to fish with me, to travel places my mom didn't like to go. He loved to ride our horses, and he loved me."

Hearing herself say her childhood fantasies out loud made her feel ridiculous and embarrassed, and she turned her head away from the serious dark eyes listening so intently. "What time is it? I need to get showered. Get ready to go to the clinic."

"In a moment." A large, gentle hand nudged her gaze back to his. "So you met him after your mother died. And he wasn't anything like your imaginary dad."

"At first, I thought he was. I was so thrilled

to meet him, and he seemed like everything I'd ever dreamed he'd be. So handsome for a man in his fifties, well-groomed, with an easy, charming smile. He told me he hadn't known about me until my mother died, when her lawyer contacted him about some money in her will. Said he felt terrible he hadn't been part of my life growing up, but that he couldn't wait to make up for all the time we'd lost together." She shut her eyes, hating to think about how gullible she'd been. In some ways, still the little girl who'd long dreamed of her superhero dad. When she opened them, she could see Enzo's were still warm and sympathetic, but getting a little hard again, too. Smart man knew this story wasn't going anywhere good.

She was silent a long moment, but Enzo didn't speak. Just ran his hand slowly up and down her side, over her hip and back, not in a sensual way, but in a caring, soothing way. Giving her time. And that comforting touch made her want to talk about it after all.

She sucked in a breath and forged on. "He

started coming around all the time, four or five times a week. We rode the horses together. Went on quite a few excursions. He seemed so interested in my nursing career, even sometimes came to a few of the architectural review meetings that I'd taken over for my mom, saying he wanted to support her passion, too. He was fun and exciting and I just felt so blessed to have finally met him. I'd lost my mom, but, after all these years, God had helped me find my dad."

"And then what happened?"

"He told me about a project he needed money for. Just a loan, to help him refurbish a few old homes he'd bought in another state. It was a lot of money, but I knew my mom would have wanted that, too. So I gave it to him."

"Oh, *tesoro*." The hand cupping her face was full of tenderness. "I'm guessing that was the last you saw of the money."

"The money, and my father." It angered her that it still hurt. She didn't even know the man, really. They shared only genes. So how could she let his dishonesty, his manipulation, his lack of moral character, hurt her at all? "Once he had the money, he disappeared. No more visits, no more telling me how happy he was to have me in his life. I soon found out through my mom's lawyer that she'd been paying him money for years to stay away, and when it stopped coming, that's when he found out she'd died. I have no idea if she paid him because she didn't want to see him, or if she knew her teen crush had turned out to be a gambler and a con man, or what. All I know is that she didn't want him to be part of my life. And I feel so stupid that I fell for the charade and for his lies."

"What a terrible thing for you to have to go through." The way he tucked her face against his neck and hugged her close felt so good, she found herself clinging to him. Hungrily soaking in the warmth and comfort he offered. "But you must tell yourself what Dante and I eventually learned. Our father's cold, selfish heart isn't the way it is because of anything we did, and no amount of love from our mother could've changed him. That's true for you, too. You wanted and deserved a good father who loved you, and it's his loss that he will never have the kind of relationship with you that you could have offered him. I'd feel sorry for him if I didn't want to beat the hell out of him."

"Thank you." Trust him to make her smile, even as she thought about how much she hated being used by the man. "If he shows up again wanting more money, can I give him your address as the place to pick it up, so you can punch his lights out?"

"It would be my pleasure. As is this, *mia belleza.*" He ran his hand down her hip again, before pulling her thigh over his. It was very apparent that their serious conversation hadn't affected his libido, and even as she was thinking they were going to be late for work, she wrapped her leg farther around him, tangled her fingers in his hair, and kissed him.

Bing-bong. The jarring sound was so loud, she jumped and nearly knocked her skull into the huge, carved wood headboard as she clutched her hand to her chest. "What was that?"

He frowned and sat up. "The doorbell. Is there another UWWHA nurse coming to stay here?"

"Not until next month, as far as I know." She hated to leave the sizzling warmth that had been zinging between them, but maybe it was for the best. "Saved by the bell, maybe? Otherwise we might have had an annoyed line of patients at the clinic before we even got there."

He responded with a heated grin as the bell gonged again, and she slid out of the bed to shove on her robe and see who the heck could be ringing.

"I'll get it." Enzo was putting his pants on with some difficulty, since his body apparently hadn't figured out they weren't doing *that* after all.

"I have my robe on already. Besides, I don't want to get a bad reputation around here with a sexy, half-naked man answering my door. Be right back."

She ran her hands through the current mess on her head as she trotted down the stone stairs, not wanting to look as if she'd just gotten lucky, even though she sure had last night. Very, very lucky. The giant door was heavy, and she slowly pulled it open to see a man standing there, formally dressed in a suit and tie and carrying a briefcase.

"May I help you?"

"Are you Aubrey Henderson?"

"Yes."

"The owner of this house has informed the UWWHA about this but wants to let you, as the current tenant, know personally, as well."

"Know what?"

"This property is almost in contract with a new buyer. The funding will be finalized within the next few days. When the purchase is complete, I'm afraid this home will no longer be available to rent, as it will go under construction immediately. The UWWHA tells me they will be contacting you about new housing. My client is giving you a three-day notice to be moved out. You will be refunded your rent accordingly."

He pulled several papers from his briefcase to hand to her, but Aubrey could barely see them as she reached for them with icy hands. All she was seeing was Enzo's determined face when he said he'd do anything he could to save the house he'd grown up in. All she was hearing was his voice telling her how much he loved this home.

Her voice shook with the big question she needed answered. "May I ask who the new buyer is?"

"Proviso Hotels. They will do a magnificent job remodeling this run-down place. You will have to come stay here again when it's finished. I am sure you will marvel at its transformation to the kind of new and modern hotel tourists will love."

CHAPTER TEN

"I TOLD YOU to sell those a week ago! Why aren't I seeing the funds as available in the account yet?"

Enzo paced his small office in the clinic, worry and frustration gnawing at his gut. Was Leonardo inept? Hadn't he made it clear to the man that he needed to immediately liquidate the assets that he'd outlined in detail?

"I did sell them. I don't know why it's not showing up as cash yet, but I'll find out right now."

"Find out sooner than right now. I need to know exactly how much more I need to outbid Proviso so I can figure out a way to get the rest by tomorrow."

He flicked through the reams of papers he'd pulled from his briefcase and laid on his desk at the clinic. He leaned his palms on his desk as he did, fighting a sickening feeling of impending defeat. Never before had he brought this kind of work to the clinic. Had always tried to keep his medical work separate from the vineyards and wineries he and Dante helped operate, and from his other business investments.

But today wasn't the day to care about that kind of separation. Desperate times called for desperate measures, as the saying went, and if he had to stare at the numbers and what else could be quickly sold to get fast cash in between seeing patients, that was what he'd have to do. Maybe there was some solution he wasn't seeing yet. Or maybe there was no solution, and his fight would end in failure, which he'd refused, until this moment, to believe could really happen.

In the midst of his intense concentration, he heard a soft knock on his office door. *"Entra."*

"Enzo."

He looked up to see Aubrey staring at him, her fingers twining anxiously together as if she had some bad news.

"What is it? Someone I need to see?"

"No. The last couple of patients have all had simple problems I could take care of without bothering you."

"Then…?"

"I want to talk to you about your house."

"Aubrey." For some inexplicable reason, just looking at her sweetly earnest face helped his lungs breathe a little easier. Which made no sense. Her caring and warmth and beauty weren't going to save his mother's house. The house she'd loved so much, that he had, too, and that he'd so wanted to keep forever. The house he'd never dreamed would be lost to him in yet another self-ish sweep by his father.

Her worried eyes stayed glued to his for a long moment before she spoke again. "Your house. We need to talk."

"I appreciate that you care. I do, more than you know." And the truth of that loosened the tense knots bunching in every muscle. "But talking isn't going to fix this problem, *bellezza*. Money is going to fix this problem, and I'm doing all I can to get it together in time to save it."

"Well, that's what I want to talk about." She licked her lips, and just as he was going to tell her not to worry, that it wasn't her problem to stress about, Nora swept into the room.

"Franca Onofrio just called. She said Carlo looks very ill, but he is refusing to go to the hospital to see what the problem is. Are you able to go see him today?"

"You want me to go by myself while you work on this?" Aubrey asked. "It might be something I can handle on my own, and if not I can call you."

"A very nice offer that I appreciate. But my first responsibility is to my job and the patients in this city, and Carlo's English is hard to follow. He's diabetic and had to have one leg removed below the knee a couple years ago. I should come to see what's going on."

"All right. I'll get both our bags together and meet you out back in, what, five minutes?"

"Yes. *Grazie.*"

He watched her rush out, wondering how he could ever have been suspicious of her motives for coming to Venice, and for working in his clinic. The woman was not only beautiful and exuberant, she was all about what she could do for others, not for what others could do for her. Something not at all true about many of the women he'd dated over the years.

After gathering the items he always took on house calls, they walked through narrow passageways and over cobbled bridges on their way to Carlo's house. "Are you glad he lives close enough that we didn't need to ride on the *vaporetto*?" he asked.

"I'm slowly getting used to the water. The risk of hyperventilating the next time I'm on a boat is getting less and less, I think."

"Bene." He liked the cute way she poked fun at herself, and, since he seemed to always be looking for a reason to touch her, he put his arm around her and tugged her against him, dropping a kiss on her forehead. "You may end up buying a boat of your own when you go back home."

He'd said the words without thinking, but when they came out of his mouth it struck him how much he would miss her. The months would go by too quickly, of that he was sure. But he also knew, deep in his soul, how lucky he was to have met her for this brief time. And since he'd been given that unexpected gift, maybe that meant he'd find a way to save his mother's house, too.

"Maybe." She looked away from him and after a pause began exclaiming brightly about the various doorways she liked to admire. Too brightly, really, and he looked closer at her, wondering if she was bothered by walking so close to the canal, or if her chatter was hiding something else.

Then she abruptly stopped talking, turning to him with an odd look of determination on her face. "About your house."

"So that's what's bothering you." He pressed a lingering kiss to her soft cheek, wanting to show her how much it meant to him that she cared. "Please stop worrying about it. I hope to have some numbers in hand later today, and I need to talk to Dante about a few of our joint liquid assets, as well."

She opened her mouth to say something else, but he dropped a quick kiss to her lips before she could speak. "Here we are at the Onofrios'. It's time to get to work."

They rang the bell and within seconds Franca had opened the door for them, ushering them inside. Enzo nudged Aubrey in ahead of him, following her through the arched stone doorway that was so low, he had to duck his head beneath it.

They followed Franca to another room, listening to her talk the whole time about how stubborn Carlo was, and how he wouldn't do a thing she asked him to. Enzo smiled to himself, thinking Aubrey would have appreciated the diatribe if she understood fast Italian, but when her amused eyes met his he could tell she got the gist of it anyway. Because it was in the center of a row of houses, the interior was fairly dark, and it took a moment for his eyes to adjust before he spotted Carlo sitting in a chair in the corner.

"I hear you're not feeling too well. What's the problem?" He felt a little rude speaking in Italian when he knew Aubrey couldn't follow, but their patient's comfort was the most important thing and he'd fill her in as he could.

"I'm okay. Franca just likes to worry and nag me."

"Which makes you a lucky man."

Carlo huffed an annoyed breath, and Enzo noted how dry his lips looked. Eyes looked a little sunken, too, so he'd guess the man was very dehydrated. He switched to English. "Aubrey, please take his vital signs. Also check his blood sugars."

She nodded and went about getting his blood pressure and sugar levels while Enzo listened to his chest. "Have you been taking your insulin the way you're supposed to?"

"Yes. Well, not this week, because I ran out."

"You ran out?" Enzo looked at him in surprise. "You know how important it is to keep your insulin levels on target. Did you—"

Franca interrupted him to loudly scold her husband, even smacking him on the shoulder as he shook his head and apparently tuned her out. Enzo glanced over to see Aubrey's eyebrows raised at the argument, and he gave her a quick grin. He'd been taking care of both of them for quite a while and couldn't remember a single time when they hadn't gotten into it over something.

"Aubrey, what's his sugar reading?"

She peered at the monitor, then her mouth dropped open as she stared up at him. "Top reading is five hundred, and it's over that."

Enzo cursed under his breath and turned to the fighting couple, needing to get this thing moving before Carlo got any worse. "You two do know I'm charging you by the minute, don't you?" He said it with a grin and this time it was his arm that Franca whacked. "In all seriousness, Carlo, your sugars are way high. Your potassium is high, and your sodium is low. Since you don't have any insulin in the house, and since you're obviously dehydrated, too, I want you to go to the hospital to get insulin right away, and some fluids."

"I don't want to go to the hospital. Franca will go get my insulin, and I'll be fine."

"I'm not arguing with you about this. I'm calling the ambulance boat, and you're going."

The man looked mulish, as if he was going to argue some more, but apparently could tell Enzo meant business and just scowled. Enzo quickly called the ambulance with the information, then turned to Franca, telling her about how soon they'd arrive. "I'll come back in a couple days to check on him. And please get his insulin prescription filled right away."

Thanking him, and nicely including Aubrey in her nods, she told them to wait a moment, returning with a bag of cookies she insisted they take. "You'll love Franca's biscotti," he said to Aubrey as they headed out the door. "Maybe we should take a coffee break to enjoy them with." Taking a short break with Aubrey, away from the clinic and the financial statements hanging over his head in his office, sounded better than good.

"I thought you had more paperwork you had to deal with."

"An hour isn't going to make a difference." He looked at her and realized how badly he needed

198 BABY SURPRISE FOR THE DOCTOR PRINCE

and wanted a break that included spending real time with her. "There's no doubt in my mind that an hour with you would boost my spirits."

"Sounds like a lot of responsibility, Dr. Affini, but you know what? I just might have an idea on what would cheer you up."

Bright sunshine poured down on them as they walked down the canal toward one of Enzo's favorite coffee shops. He wrapped his arm around Aubrey's waist, and just tugging her close was enough to boost his spirits already.

"Isn't it a beautiful day? Not a cloud in the sky." The smile she turned to him was wide and full of the joy he'd seen in her so often, but at the same time he could tell it was shadowed with concern. "Though I know it's hard to enjoy when you have such a tough situation going on right now. I can't tell you how sorry I am about that."

"I'll figure it out." He had no idea if that was true, but what was the point of her worrying, too?

They moved from the narrow passage to a walkway by one of the small canals. Children were kicking a ball back and forth across it, laughing and good-naturedly arguing when the ball plopped into the water.

"Is this a game you played as a kid?" she asked, holding her hand above her eyes to shield them from the high, midday sun.

"Dante and our friends were always cooking up new games to play when older games got boring, but I'm not sure about this one. Looks like they're trying to either catch the ball, or kick it into one of the boats."

"I can just see you as a boy playing here."

"Because I seem childlike to you?"

"Um…that would be a definite no." There was a teasing smile on her lips as she looked up at him, but her gaze didn't seem smiling at all. It seemed hot and filled with sexy thoughts, and he was so mesmerized by it, he didn't see the ball heading straight toward his head until it smacked right into him, practically knocking him sideways.

"Oh, my gosh!" Aubrey rested her soft palm against his temple. It throbbed and hurt like crazy, but he wasn't going to let her know that. "Are you all right?"

"Good thing it hit my head. Dante would say it's the hardest part of me."

"That's because he doesn't know what's *really* the hardest part of you."

That made a laugh burst out of his chest, which made his head ache even worse. He leaned toward her, loving the coy look on her face that was making that sometimes hard part of him start to do exactly what she was talking about. "Ah, *bellezza*. I'm more than happy to—"

The boys interrupted him with a spate of shouts, and he turned to see the ball floating down the canal, out of their reach.

"They want you to fetch the ball, I'm guessing?"

"Your Italian is getting good, Ms. Henderson."

"Don't have to speak Italian to figure that out." She grinned. "Need help?"

"No. I'll use a fishing net from one of these boats. Be right back."

It took just a few minutes, and as he was shaking water from the ball before he carried it back he heard the children screaming, then Aubrey shrieking.

What the…? He looked up just in time to see Aubrey's white skirt flying into the air in front of her fluttering legs and shoed feet before she did a belly flop straight into the canal.

CHAPTER ELEVEN

MIO DIO. WITH HIS heart pounding straight up into his throat, Enzo sprinted to the spot she'd gone in, about to jump in himself when Aubrey's head came back up. Her soaking hair was streaming into her eyes and he could tell she was catching her breath, but was obviously treading water as she held a crying, very small little girl in her arms. She was talking in a breathless but soothing voice to the child, pushing the girl's black hair out of her eyes as she did. Since Aubrey wasn't using her hands to swim, she must have been doing some kind of scissor kick, as she was making her way over to the wall of the canal. Several children were standing there ready to grab the little one, but Enzo stepped in front of them, pulled her from Aubrey's arms, handed her to one of the older kids, then reached for Aubrey.

Hardly able to breathe, as if he'd been the one underwater, he shoved his hands deep down to grasp her waist. Lifting her out of the canal and high into his arms, he smashed her tightly against his chest as he pressed his cheek to hers. After barely starting up again from the scare of seeing her go into that water, his heart now slammed hard against hers, and he wasn't sure if it was her shaking from the chill of the water, or him shaking, or both of them.

"What were you thinking? Why in the world did you do that? Can you even swim?"

"I told you, I can swim. I swim in pools all the time. It's dark lake and river water that scares me."

"Which the canal is. *Dio!*" He lifted his head just enough to look in her eyes, and that they were shining and happy made him want to shake her. "Seeing you go in that water took ten years off my life."

"I'm sorry." From the gleam in her eyes, it didn't seem like she was sorry at all. "But we need to check on the little one. Hold on."

She pulled herself from his arms, smoothed the rest of her wet hair from her face, and crouched down to the child, who Enzo could now see was probably only three years old, or so. She was still crying, but just a little, sniffling and nodding and looking a little shy as Aubrey spoke to her. Enzo had a feeling the child had no idea what Aubrey was saying, but the way she smiled at her was a universal language, wasn't it?

Aubrey gave her a quick hug as the older children thanked her, picked up the ball Enzo had dropped when he'd fished them both out of the canal, and went off to play again.

"Are you done playing hero for today?" He folded his arms across his chest, wanting her to know that, even though it had turned out well, he still couldn't believe she'd put herself at risk like that, scaring him to death in the process, when it should have been him going in after the child.

"For today, yes." She grinned at him. "Oh, come on. If you'd been standing there, you would have gone in, too."

"In case you hadn't noticed, I was plenty close

enough to have done the jumping in. Not to mention that I'm not afraid of water, which might have sent you into a panic, which you know as well as I do is often the reason people drown."

"You're being dramatic. I knew you were close by." She waved her hand before she used it to pull his wet, clinging shirt away from his skin. "But I am sorry I got you all wet. And that you were worried."

Exactly how worried still shocked him. He couldn't deny that the instant terror he'd felt had been a little unnecessary. Extreme, even. And what exactly that said, he didn't want to analyze too much.

"We should get back to the clinic." His voice was gruff, and he knew the arm he wrapped around her waist was a little too tight, but that was too bad. He needed to feel it there. Needed to hold her close.

That closeness had him finally thinking less about how upset he'd been and what had just happened and more about her and her discomfort when he felt her shivering against him. He stopped to rub his hands briskly over the goose bumps on her arms. "You're cold. How about I get you a water taxi back to the house? You can take a hot shower, change into dry clothes, and relax without worrying about coming back to work."

"I'm fine." She ran her hands up his damp shirt to wrap them around his neck as she pressed her smiling mouth against his as he folded her close, feeling the tension of the past five minutes slip away as he held her. "I'll take a shower at the clinic. Get into a dry uniform there. But you're sweet to want to take care of me."

Surprising was the word he'd use, since wanting to take care of her seemed extremely important. Remembering all they'd done in that shower got his heart rate cranking all over again, and he kissed her again, a little deeper this time. When he came up for air, he heard some giggling and realized a few of the kids were watching.

"The Italian version of the peanut gallery," he said drily as he took her hand. "Let's get you into that shower, and, Aubrey?"

"Yes?"

"Warning you that I just might use having my clothes wet, too, as a great excuse to join you there."

With the last patient of the day gone and the clinic closed, Aubrey paced in front of Enzo's office door. After they'd returned yesterday to dry off after her canal plunge, he'd spent most of the afternoon in there. Today, he'd been closeted inside the entire time he wasn't seeing patients, studying spreadsheets, making long private phone calls, and disappearing periodically. Clearly, he hadn't found a solution yet.

She wasn't sure she should disturb him, and even less sure what exactly she should say, even though she'd been pondering it for two solid days. Thinking about her forced move date from his house—former house—tomorrow. He'd been so busy with it, the other doctor had come to the clinic for a few hours to take over some of the patient load. And while Dr. Lambre was nice enough, and a good doctor, work hadn't been the same without Enzo patiently working along with her. Exuding his potent charm and sending that impish grin to some patients, while getting gently tough—a seeming oxymoron he amazingly managed—with the most difficult patients.

Despite their rocky start when she'd first returned to Venice, she'd come to see that he was a good man. A very special man. And because he was, and because she wanted to help him and *could* help him, she stiffened her spine and forced herself to knock on the door.

"Entra."

Holding her breath, she pushed open the door, expecting him to be looking up at her. Instead, his head was lowered to the papers in front of him, a deep frown creased his brow, and, even worse, his fingertips were pressed against his closed eyes.

That utter picture of stress and despair made her heart squeeze hard in her chest. Made her wish she were a huge, burly man who could go find his father and beat the heck out of him for doing this to his son, the way Enzo had said he would do to her own father if he could. But it also made what she had to say easier.

"I'm sorry to bother you. But can we talk for a minute?"

His hands dropped to the desk as he looked up and gave her a smile. If you could call it a smile, because it was a forced, gray shadow of his usual, adorable grin. "Of course. I'm sorry that I've been busy and…absent. I hope working with Antonio has been okay?"

"It's been fine." She sucked in another fortifying breath and forged on. "I know you have a lot going on, but can we maybe get a drink somewhere in the fresh air? It's a beautiful evening, and I know you probably need a break."

The eyes that looked back at her were dark and scarily lacking all their usual warmth and vivacity, but she could see him trying hard to push past the darkness obviously consuming him right now.

"A break and a drink sounds good. Better than good, if it's with you."

Relief weakened her knees, and she walked to

his desk to reach out her hand. "You promised to be my Venetian tour guide, His Excellency Dr. Prince Affini. Where's the best place close to here for a perfect Italian Bellini?"

"Bellinis are a bit fruity for my taste, but, if that's what you want, I know of a good place a bit past all the tourist spots, but not too far."

That it had taken a long moment for him to grasp her hand worried her, and the half smile he gave her worried her, too, but she'd get him out of the clinic any way she could. Because they had important things to talk about, and maybe those things would bring the smile she'd come to love back to his handsome face.

The sun was hiding behind thick clouds on the horizon as they walked along the Riva Degli Schiavoni toward the restaurant and bar Enzo had suggested with obvious reluctance. Aubrey pondered when and how to broach the subject they needed to talk about. The evening was alive with tourists walking the promenade, and vendors of all kinds were working to sell their wares, but one in particular caught her eye.

"Those watercolors are beautiful, don't you think? Do you mind if we look? I'm going to need a few souvenirs to take home."

She didn't really want to think about souvenirs, and about going home, but hoped maybe a benign distraction and conversation would be a good thing before she tackled what she really wanted to talk about over that Bellini.

"You do realize there are dozens of artists selling paintings of Venice everywhere you go here." The smile Enzo sent her was better, a little more real, than the one they'd started this excursion with, and her heart lifted a little that it was a start.

"I know. But I might find the perfect one when I least expect it, right? Why wait until the day before I'm leaving for the States?"

He seemed to look at her a long time before he answered. "Yes. Why wait?"

Her stomach jittered with nerves, and she made some lighthearted conversation about all the touristy stuff for sale, trying to bring them back to their former relaxed banter. As they walked along there were artists who were painting at the same time they chatted to tourists. Others sat on folding chairs, looking a little bored as people walked by to admire their work.

"I can guess which artists are selling more, can't you?" Just as she said it in a grinning undertone her heart jolted in her chest at one of the watercolors on display.

"Look!" So surprised, she felt a little breathless as she tugged him toward the various canvases propped on easels next to stacks of other artwork. "It's your house. Your beautiful house. Right there, in the painting!"

"Sì." His arm wrapped around her waist and held her close to his hard body as he looked down at her, and not the painting. "It's a very famous house. One often photographed as being quintessential Venetian, standing tall and proud in the middle of two canals. You've already noticed its unique design. One of the many important buildings that are part of our history. Part of the fortunes and extravagance of nobles and aristocracy from bygone days."

She stared up at him as his dark gaze met hers. For those who might not know him, his expression seemed impassive. Matter of fact. But she knew differently. Knew that beyond the calm facade he tried to portray to others lay a world of emotion. A deep love for this city and his ancestral home and, yes, for his mother. A love that went far beyond the connection Aubrey felt to her house in Massachusetts that her mother had held dear to her heart. The home in this painting, this amazing place built more than seven hundred years ago, the house he'd grown up in, could never be replaced. Because it was irreplaceable.

That certain conviction gave her the strength she needed. "Are we getting close to that Bellini? Because I'm dying of thirst."

"That's surprising, since you decided to drink some canal water yesterday." He dropped a smiling kiss to her forehead. "Don't worry, it's not much farther."

Aubrey was glad that an outside table set slightly apart from the others was available for them. Sitting there looking out over the darkening water, she clutched her cold glass and glanced at Enzo as she breathed in the lagoon air for strength. Nerves jittered in every muscle, and, while it seemed ridiculous, she knew it wasn't because what she was about to say was important to only her. She knew it was important to him, too, and also knew it was going to be very hard to convince him to accept her help. And learning exactly where everything stood and what weighed in the balance had to come first.

"So, tell me what progress you've made on buying the house back."

His eyes met hers, dark and brooding and so somber, she wanted to reach for him before they said another word. She tightened her fingers on her drink and bit her tongue to keep from touching him or saying anything else, because, as hard as it was to be patient, she knew she had to give him a chance to talk.

"If you're wanting me to say that all is fixed and I've bought the house back and you can keep living there, I'm afraid I can't."

"The house sale is due to close day after to-morrow."

"This I know. Your point?"

"I want to help."

His chest heaved in a deep sigh as he reached for her hand. "And I thank you for that. But this is a battle I must finish on my own."

"Why? Are you too proud to accept help?"

"Aubrey. There is no way for you to help." He said her name on a long breath, a quiet defeat in his voice as he brought her hand to his mouth, holding his lips there until she loosened it to hold his cheek in her palm instead.

"Maybe that's because you haven't yet listened to what I have to say."

A sad smile that was so unlike any Enzo smile she'd seen before touched his lips. "Then of course I'm more than willing to hear it. You have much wisdom in that amazing brain of yours."

"Thank you. But this isn't about wisdom." She licked her lips and stared into the brown eyes she'd come to care about so much, praying he'd accept her proposal. "This is about practicality and business, pure and simple."

"You have a business proposition for me?" This time, his smile looked a little more real. "Talented nurse, architectural historian, child rescuer, and a businesswoman, too? I'm all ears."

"I'm glad to hear that. How much money do you still need to outbid Proviso?"

"About one hundred thirty-five thousand euro. Which today is approximately one hundred fifty thousand dollars."

"I'm guessing you're having a hard time getting it by tomorrow."

"You already know that most of the land we own is held in trust, and I don't have access to it to sell it. I've liquidated a number of my assets, but many others aren't liquid. And I can't take out more loans, because that would be irresponsible. I have to think about the people who work for me on my various properties. Dipping into the accounts that pay them would be wrong. So I'm coming up short but am still working on it."

"But it's not looking good."

"No." The dark eyes that met hers communicated much more than that simple word. "It's not looking good."

"I have a solution." She drew breath, afraid to say it because she had a bad feeling he'd flatly say no. "I'd like to give one hundred fifty thousand dollars to the fund you have set up to buy it back."

His stunned expression would have been comical if there had been anything funny about the situation he faced. "What? No."

"Yes." She reached for his hand. "I love that house, too, and I've lived there barely two weeks. I can't imagine you losing it when you and your mother grew up there. You know that saving historical homes is important to me and was important to *my* mother. Seeing her money, which is now mine, go to keeping a historic landmark from being gutted would make her happy. And it would make me happy, too."

"Aubrey." He shook his head as he stared at her. "I can't accept that. It might take me a long time to pay you back."

"You wouldn't have to pay it back. It would come out of the same fund I accessed to adopt the fresco. That my mother set up years ago for preserving homes like yours. Well, not exactly, because there's nothing like yours in the US." She smiled, wanting to make him smile, too. To see that it really was all right for him to accept her offer.

He lifted her hand and brought it to his lips as he had before, then leaned across the table to kiss her mouth. Soft and sweet and so full of emotion, it felt as if the kiss sneaked all the way into her heart. She clutched at his shoulders to draw him closer, and when their lips finally parted, their eyes met in the silent connection she'd felt since the first moment they met.

"Say yes," she breathed.

His lips brushed hers as he shook his head. "No, *tesoro*. I can't. I'm moved more than I can say by your generous offer, but this is my battle to fight."

"So you won't let anyone else on the battlefield to fight with you?"

"Not you, not anyone except my brother and my bankers. But there is one thing you can do for me."

"What?"

He held her face in his hands, and the eyes meeting hers held something like awe along with the heat that made her quiver. "Let me spend one more night in the house with you. One more sweet night with a special woman to join the many important memories I already have there. Please?"

As if he had to ask. And maybe, just maybe, after another night of lovemaking she could change his mind. She pressed her lips to his and whispered, "Your wish is my command, Your Excellency."

CHAPTER TWELVE

ENZO WAS GLAD that the clinic had been filled with patients all morning, and that Aubrey hadn't been there with him. Focusing on work was probably the only way to take his mind off the reality of what was happening today. That it was moving day for Aubrey, with the sale of the house going through soon. His stomach had churned about it for days now, but today he felt more resigned to the harsh reality that it would soon no longer be the house it had been for so many centuries, but transformed into some monstrosity instead.

He knew that making love with Aubrey again last night was part of the reason he felt calmer about it. Something about being with her had filled the empty hollow in his chest when he'd finally seen there was almost no chance that he could buy the house in time. Took some of the sadness away, too. Even some of the exhaustion he'd felt when it became painfully clear that defeat was imminent.

That she'd offered him so much money to help him blew his mind. Free and clear and with no strings attached just because she knew it was important to him. Yes, he knew she liked the house, and was fascinated by its history, but that could be said of any number of houses in Venice ready to go on the chopping block, and probably a few of the older homes in the States that her mother had cared about.

No, he knew she'd offered it because she cared about him. Which humbled him. Overwhelmed him. And when he'd made love with her last night, his heart had felt strangely light and heavy at the same time. Had felt a reverence for her when he'd kissed her and touched her that was completely foreign to his existence. Emotions he'd never felt or experienced before, and he knew he was teetering dangerously close to loving her.

And that would be bad. Very bad for her. He

knew it but selfishly couldn't bring himself to end things just yet. They both knew there was an end date for their relationship, didn't they? She had a life and home to go back to in the States after she was done with her tenure here. Just thinking about how much he would miss her when she left stabbed his heart before it had even happened. But he knew that a few more months with her would be more than worth the pain and emptiness he'd feel after she was gone.

The ring of his cell phone startled him and he fished it out of his pocket to see it was Leonardo. A few days ago he might have gotten hyped up about a phone call, wondering if there was good news, but today he knew the conversation would be more about closure. About what to do with the funds they'd liquidated into cash now that they couldn't buy the house.

"Have you seen this, Enzo?" Leonardo's voice was loud and excited and Enzo strode into his office, wondering what the man could possibly be so excited about.

"What?"

"There's enough money in the fund!"

"What do you mean?"

"There's been a big cash transfer. We've done it! I've sent it all over to the Realtor and lawyer to get the transaction expedited and completed, hopefully today. If all goes well, that house will be yours again by tomorrow, Enzo. Congratulations."

He dropped down into his chair, and a sudden, sickening feeling joined the cautious optimism that swirled around his gut. "Where did this cash transfer come from?"

"It's from a trust in the States. Henderson LLC. Do you know who that is?"

Dio.

He scrubbed his hand down his face. What should he do? Should he accept Aubrey's incredibly generous gift? Let the sale go through? Getting to keep that house and eventually renovating it would all be due to Aubrey if he did.

A deep sigh left his aching chest. He wanted to. *Dio*, he wanted to more than he could say. But what kind of person would that make him? Taking that kind of money from a woman so incredibly special, so amazing, so loving and giving, while offering her absolutely nothing in return would be all kinds of wrong.

He wasn't a fool. He knew women. He knew Aubrey was coming to care for him the way he was her, even though he didn't deserve it. That she was on the verge of loving him, which last night had proven to both of them.

He couldn't let himself be the kind of rat his father was, using her to his own ends without being able to commit to her. Loving her while she was here, yes, but he couldn't love her forever because that would just end up in pain and sorrow for Aubrey, and she deserved so much more than that.

She deserved the world from a man who wasn't a bad bet, and he knew at that moment with absolute certainty that he had to save her from him. He already wanted to keep her close. The way he felt about her filled his chest and heart in a way he'd never experienced before. Big and overwhelming, and because of that he could see himself making promises he couldn't keep.

He absolutely could not selfishly hurt her that way.

No. He'd send her money back to her and keep his distance. Work opposite shifts, and have Antonio work with her instead of him. Maybe he'd even take some vacation time away from the clinic, go see how the vineyards and wineries were doing. Spend time with his brother and get to know Shay.

Losing both Aubrey and the house at the same time made his heart feel as if it had turned into a heavy stone weight, but it was the only choice he could make.

He refused to be the man his father was. He would not be the man who broke Aubrey Henderson's beautiful heart.

"We can't accept the money, Leonardo. Don't argue with me, please. I'm telling you we can't. Transfer it back to the trust with our thanks and regrets."

* * *

"*Buongiorno*, Aubrey." Antonio Lambre gave her a smile as she walked into the clinic. "No patients here yet, so take your time changing."

"Thanks, Dr. Lambre. I'll be ready shortly." She moved to the locker room, and her stomach lurched the way it had the past seven days. A rising anger had joined her confusion and the sick feeling in her belly every day that she'd come to the clinic and Enzo hadn't been there.

She knew he'd been in Venice the entire past week, because of course she'd had to look at the work schedule. Which he'd carefully written to have them work on days opposite one another. She'd called him a couple times, too, to see how he was feeling now that the house sale had gone through and ask if he was happy and if he was going to move there, since the UWWHA nurses weren't renting it anymore. To ask if he wanted to come see the awful little modern apartment they'd stuck her in and laugh about it.

And how unbearably humiliating was all that? Calling him like a moonstruck teen, even though it was now beyond clear he was avoiding her big-time. Embarrassing beyond belief that she'd secretly hoped he'd ask her if she wanted to move back to his house, now that he owned it free and clear. The paperwork from her financial advisor and lawyers had come through showing he'd happily accepted the money he'd claimed he didn't want. And she'd seen in the newspaper just that morning that the house was officially back in the royal family again.

Was it possible that he was just super busy with finalizing everything? But how could he be so busy that he wouldn't even call her? Wouldn't want to celebrate with her?

She moved toward the new week's schedule, hating to have to see how he'd written it this time, at the same time stupidly hoping she was wrong, that he wasn't avoiding her, that there was some other explanation. That they'd be working together again. Sharing picnics again. Making love again. Then stared when she saw he wasn't on the schedule at all.

"Just step right in here, Madame Durand. The nurse will be with you in a moment."

Aubrey ran her suddenly icy hands down her skirt and stepped to the hallway as Nora closed the exam-room door.

"I have a patient for you, Aubrey. Room two."

She nodded and licked her lips to moisten her dry mouth. Her heart was thumping so hard she could hear it in her ears, and she was having so much trouble breathing she had to suck in air twice before she spoke. "Nora. I see that Dr. Affini isn't on the schedule for this next week. Do you know why?"

"He took some time off to go to his home in Tuscany. Left a couple days ago. He has property there, you know, and needs to check on it now and then, I think. He hasn't been there for quite some time. I'm not sure how long he'll be gone."

"Thank you." She needed to get out of there for a minute before she saw her patient. She stumbled out the back door and breathed in the lagoon air she'd come to love almost as much as she loved Enzo.

Lying, deceiving rat that he was. Because the only explanation for his suddenly steering clear of her, even leaving for another part of the country, which he apparently hadn't done for a long while, was loud and painfully clear.

Funny how he'd been so unpleasant to her until the meeting where he'd learned she'd donated money to restore the fresco. Suddenly he was apologizing, then all nice and charming the following day. He'd accused her of having an agenda? What a joke.

He'd gotten what he wanted, then he'd taken off, just like her father.

Barely able to swallow the bitter taste of that reality, she forced herself to go back to do her job. But as she walked inside the clinic she thought about all he'd said about his mother. How she'd loved his father even though she knew he didn't love her back, and here Aubrey was, doing the exact same thing.

Pining for a man who didn't truly care about her.

She stood there a long moment, facing that horrifying realization. Pictured herself working in this clinic day after day, checking the schedule over and over again. Knowing she'd dread seeing him at the same time she craved it, might even forgive him the way she had after he'd been so nasty just a few weeks ago. Thinking about how easily she'd done that forced her to see what had to happen.

She couldn't stay in Venice any longer.

She had to go home. As soon as possible. And yes, that made her weak and pathetic, but being those things was better than staying in this city she loved without the man she'd pitifully come to love, too. Thinking of him as she walked along the canals and looked at all the fascinating buildings, hearing the sexy rumble of his voice as he talked about it all. Wishing he were beside her as she rode the *vaporetto*, telling her how brave she was. Missing his touch, his kisses, the way he'd looked at her and held her with such an incredible intimacy, she'd fallen headlong in love with a lie.

Except there was one thing he'd said that hadn't

been a lie. He'd been absolutely truthful when he'd told her he was a bad bet for any woman. She could only hope her battered, deluded heart would eventually truly believe it.

Enzo tipped his forehead against the airplane window and looked down at the city he loved, waiting for the smile that always came as he did. Instead, a peculiar mix of anxiety and nervous anticipation roiled in his belly. There was a sense of grief, too, over losing his mother's house, but he'd worked hard to put that behind him. To roam the beautiful hillsides of the Affini estates, to walk the vineyards and enjoy time in the villa he still owned that had always been an enjoyable respite for him and Dante and his mother when they'd needed a short break from the close quarters and summer heat of Venice.

He tried to conjure the bit of happiness he felt that his brother, at least, had saved his own properties from their father's selfishness. Dante hadn't planned it, but clearly it had been meant to be for him to have a child with Shay. And Enzo had to admit he was looking forward to playing with his niece or nephew in the same rolling hills he and Dante had played in as kids.

How to handle being back at the clinic and having to see Aubrey was something he hadn't figured out yet. Scheduling Antonio to work the same shifts she did had worked in the short-term, but he knew there would come a time when that wasn't feasible. So then what?

Working with her again would be sweet torture. He wanted to look into her beautiful eyes, see her dazzling smile, listen to her laugh. But he knew not reaching to touch her and hold her, not kissing her or wanting to enjoy more time with her on the lagoon or anywhere else would be nearly impossible. He honestly didn't know if he could do it, so where did that leave him?

In serious trouble, that was where.

He leaned his head back against the seat and closed his eyes. Aubrey. How had she become so deeply nestled inside him in such a short period of time? She was on his mind as he rode the water taxi from the airport, looking out over the island where they'd picnicked and laughed and kissed. He thought of her as he watched the cormorants fly and dive for fish, remembering the oil smudged on her beautiful face, her happy smile as they'd rescued the bird. The way she'd clung to him on both his small boat and the *vaporetto*, forcing herself to face her fear, then actually leaping into the canal to save that little girl.

Whenever he'd been gone from Venice for a while, the lagoon air filling his lungs on the taxi ride from the airport was another thing that usually made him smile. This time, the air felt thick and heavy instead of invigorating.

He slowly walked from the *vaporetto* stop to his house, feeling as if he had lead weights in his feet. Aubrey was still on his mind as he passed the old doors that fascinated her, and he wondered where the UWWHA had put her up after she'd had to move from his old home. Was she happy there? Finding new places in Venice to explore without him? He hoped she was. Hoped she didn't miss him the way he was missing her.

Which brought back to mind the huge problem of working with her again.

How was he going to handle it?

Piles of mail that his housekeeper had stacked on the old wooden table in his foyer needed attention and he started sifting through them to see which seemed the most urgent. A larger envelope delivered by certified mail was tucked in between bills and letters and catalogs, and he tore it open. Then stared.

It was the deed to his mother's house.

What the…? His breath backed up in his lungs, and it felt as if his heart stopped for a long moment before lurching back into rhythm. He stared at it again, but there it was in black and white. His name on the deed. He owned the house.

How had this happened?

A letter was enclosed in the envelope, too, and he slowly slipped it out to read it. Then read it again. His lawyer outlined the details of the transaction and the final price, ending the letter with a hearty congratulations on his success getting the funding together in time.

Except he hadn't. Which left only one explanation. Somehow Aubrey's money hadn't been sent back to her, after all.

Head spinning, he hoped he was wrong. That something else had come through in time. He practically staggered to a chair and dropped into it, pulling out his phone to dial Leonardo.

"Can you explain why the deed to the house is now in my name and in my possession? Can you also tell me why all this went through, and nobody bothered to tell me? Would maybe a phone call have been in order?"

"I assumed you knew. I got a copy of the letter the lawyer sent you weeks ago."

"I was out of town and didn't get my mail." Hiding away from Aubrey, and look what had happened because of his cowardice.

"Well, there was a little mix-up." Now Leonardo sounded sheepish and contrite and a little worried. "I did what you asked with the Henderson money, except I'd already transferred the fund over to the Realtor and your lawyer before I'd talked to you. Then neither of them answered my call at first, and by the time they called me back, it was a done deal. Because we—you—bought it with cash at a slightly higher price than Proviso had offered, the seller was happy to take it and run. So, um, a belated congratulations!"

Dio mio. "Leo. This is a huge problem." He rubbed his hand across his forehead as emotions ping-ponged all over the place. The house was his. For real. The house he loved more than anything. Except maybe not. The way he felt at that moment told him that maybe he loved Aubrey even more, and if he did how could he possibly accept her gift? Giving her nothing back but probably a deep disappointment in him that he wasn't the man she'd doubtless believed he was? That he wished he could be?

"Why is this such a big deal?" Leonardo asked. "If it's the money from Henderson LLC, we can always pay it back, you know. Consider that it just bought you more time to raise the money you needed. So we keep working to raise more cash over the next few months, then you can pay it back. With interest, if that's important to you.

This isn't the problem you're making it out to be, Enzo. Consider it heaven-sent, instead."

Heaven-sent. That was Aubrey, not the money, and he had to go see her right away. Talk to her about all this.

"Plan to pay the money back, Leo. I'll be working on raising it."

He hung up and called Aubrey, shocked that his hand was actually shaking as he dialed. Then everything inside was shaking, too, when it went to voice mail. He strode out the door again and headed straight to the clinic. It wouldn't close for another hour. He had no idea if she'd be there, since he'd been gone for almost three weeks, and Antonio had been doing the scheduling. But if she wasn't, at least Nora would surely know where Aubrey was living now.

He went in the back door, his stomach in knots. The exam doors were both closed, so presumably patients were inside, and he headed to the front desk to find Nora. More patients waiting to be seen sat in the few chairs, and he came up behind Nora, leaning down close to her ear.

"Can we talk for a minute?"

She looked up and her mouth dropped open in surprise. "Dr. Affini! When did you get back?"

"Just now." He lowered his voice even more. "Is Aubrey working today?"

She looked perplexed, tipping her head sideways to look up at him. "No. She apparently told the UWWHA she wanted to be reassigned somewhere else later in the year. I believe she went back to the States."

Enzo stared at her, wondering if he'd heard right. "She's not in Venice?"

"No. She left about two weeks ago. Do you want to meet the new nurse? She's—"

"I'll meet her another time." Since the world seemed to tilt on its axis, making Enzo feel a little dizzy, he'd barely been able to answer. "Do you by chance know where Aubrey lives in the States?"

"I have no idea. You could probably find out from the UWWHA." Nora was looking at him with great interest, which made him wonder what his face looked like.

"Good suggestion." He drew in a deep, shaky breath. "Thanks." His legs felt a little numb as he walked out the door, having no idea where he was even going.

Aubrey had left Venice? Gone home, or maybe even somewhere else in the States? How in the world was he going to find her? He had to clear up this mistake. Let her know how much he appreciated her help and that he'd pay her back.

He walked through the city he loved, and every step he took made him think of her. All the things she loved about it, all the things he'd loved showing her. His feet took him past the artists selling paintings of the buildings and his house and that made him think of her, too.

How had every part of this city become filled with memories of her in a matter of weeks? *Dio*, he wanted to have her there with him. Kiss her and hold her and make love with her again, but as he stood there he forced himself to realize that her being gone was for the best, taking all temptation with her. He wouldn't have to go through trying to work with her while keeping his distance, which had been torture before he'd gone to Tuscany.

She was the most special woman he'd ever been privileged to be with, and nothing had changed about that. Which also meant nothing had changed about needing to stay away from her so there was no chance he could hurt her. She deserved a man who could give her his heart and soul and a forever after, and as he stood there picturing her beautiful face and shining eyes, hearing her inquisitive questions and infectious laughter, the thought of her with someone else made him feel as if he were bleeding inside.

None of that mattered. Her feelings were what mattered. And as he stared out over the water, the deep ache in his chest he wasn't sure would ever completely go away told him that calling her would be a bad idea. Hearing her sweet voice might make him do something stupid, like beg her to come back to Venice, or let him visit her in Massachusetts or wherever she was so he could see her one more time. Touch her once more. And how selfish would that be?

No, as soon as he was able to find out from the UWWHA where she was living, he'd have his lawyer send her a letter about the transaction. Tell her that he would be returning the money with interest as soon as he had it. He'd write her a letter, too, thanking her for her generosity and telling her he wished her all the best for her life.

Somehow, he'd keep it cool and professional as he'd tried to do before, until he'd completely caved to the allure of Aubrey Henderson. Then he'd go back to his old life. Except that life now, at the clinic and this city, would hold memories of her everywhere, and he had no idea how he was going to deal with the pain of her being gone.

CHAPTER THIRTEEN

AUBREY STOOD IN the old bedroom she'd grown up in and changed out of her uniform, thinking about how mundane her life felt now. Hoped that feeling would change once some time had passed, bringing back her interest in all the places nearby she'd always loved to go. Assumed that working at the nearby hospital again would start to feel challenging and interesting instead of days she just needed to get through.

As she wandered across the grass to the stable she scolded herself for that thought. She'd had some lovely patients she'd enjoyed taking care of, and had managed to have some fun with friends, too, right? And with her old nanny, Maggie, who lived in one of the guest houses. Anyone would feel a little let down coming back to the life they'd lived for years after the adventure of living and working in a place as incredible as Venice.

Maybe it was because she'd been feeling tired. Kind of sick, really. Queasy and a little dizzy, and she hoped she wasn't coming down with some kind of stomach bug.

That must be it. Her malaise had nothing to do with Enzo Affini. Okay, maybe it did, but that just made her mad because he didn't deserve for her to be moping around about him. Wasn't worth her heart still hurting and her stomach feeling all twisted around at the way he'd used her.

How had she let herself fall in love with a mirage? A prince doctor used to having people fall all over him, and using that to his advantage, deceiving them with his charm and easy smile and a sexiness that would wow anyone?

No, it wasn't her fault. If she kept reminding herself she disliked him now, one of these days her heart would finally catch on and life would get back to normal.

Except right now, normal felt very, very dull

compared to being with a handsome, charming, manipulative man in beautiful Italy.

She made her way into the barn, waving when she saw that Maggie was at the far end, feeding one of the horses a treat. "Hey, Maggie! Going riding tonight?"

"Planning to." The nurse and nanny who had been part of the family for years beamed her sweet smile. "Want to join me?"

"Thanks, but not today. I'm not feeling too good." She put her hand to her stomach because the queasiness seemed worse. Maybe after she went back inside, she'd make herself some chicken soup or something to see if that would help.

But first, she'd say hi to one of her favorite horses. She headed to his stall to rub his nose. "Do you think I'm an idiot, Applejax? You know how my dad turned out to be a jerk. But you had no idea he was like that, did you? Should I have known? Am I just a really bad judge of character, being taken in by both of them?"

The horse bobbed his nose up and down in

agreement, and she grimaced. Yeah, maybe she was just bad at reading people, and she wondered if there were lessons on how to get better at it.

Her stomach lurched a little more, and the realization that she might actually get sick had her deciding to get back to the house sooner rather than later. But as she turned, her head strangely swam, the light seemed to glitter, then fade, and her legs felt as if they just crumpled beneath her.

Blinking open her eyes, she looked up into Maggie's anxious face just above her. It took her a second to realize she was lying flat on her back, and when she lifted her hand to her head she felt some straw stuck in her hair.

"What...what happened?"

"You fainted dead away, sweetie. About gave me a heart attack."

"Fainted? What?"

She could see Maggie looking at her closely as she helped her sit up. "Feel like you can stand now?"

"Yes. I feel okay. I can't imagine how that happened."

"Well, there could be lots of reasons. Take your time walking, and lean on me, okay?"

They slowly walked back to the house, with Maggie's arm wrapped around her waist as she'd often done when Aubrey was little. "How are you feeling now?"

"I'm fine. Really. I think I have a bug. Been feeling light-headed and queasy on and off the past couple of days."

Maggie didn't speak for a long moment, then asked, "Any chance you could be pregnant?"

"What?" She stared in disbelief that Maggie had even asked her that. "Of course not! I'm on the Pill. I mean, I did miss a couple of periods, but that happens sometimes with the one I'm taking, and, well…" Her voice faded off as a cold chill came over her that didn't have anything to do with her bug.

Surely there was no way she could be pregnant. Was there?

"You know I have all kinds of nursing supplies at my house, including a pregnancy test." She tucked Aubrey into her favorite chair and briskly plumped pillows behind her head, then got her a cold drink. "You get comfy and I'll be right back."

With her figurative nursing hat firmly in place, Maggie was speaking in a no-nonsense voice, and while Aubrey wanted to say she didn't need the test, the suddenly really scared part of her had to know.

Getting comfy wasn't possible, despite sitting in the plush chair with her feet up while she waited for Maggie. Aubrey sipped her water and thought about Enzo.

What if she really was pregnant? As Shay had gotten pregnant by Dante? What in the world would she do? And would Enzo think she'd done it on purpose, since he'd been suspicious of why she'd shown up to work at the clinic that first day?

The thought sent another cold chill sliding down her spine and made her feel even sicker than she had before.

It seemed like an eternity before Maggie got back with the test. All too soon, the answer was terrifyingly clear in the form of an intense pink dot. She stared at it for long minutes, feeling as if she might faint all over again. She sucked in deep breaths and looked into the mirror to see her shocked eyes staring back at her.

How in the world had this happened?

Somehow getting her wobbly legs to work, she finally made it back to the living room to see Maggie. The result must have been more than obvious on her face, because Maggie stood up and came to hug her.

"Ah, sweetie. Come sit down and let's talk."

"Oh, my God. What am I going to do?"

"Who is the father? Someone you like?" She gently pushed Aubrey back into the chair and patted her knee. "Is he here or in Italy?"

She stared up into Maggie's wrinkled face, and the calm, nonjudgmental way she asked the question helped Aubrey start breathing again. "He lives in Venice. He's a doctor. And a prince." *And a jerk.*

Maggie grinned. "Trust you to do it right, little one."

"Do it right? This is awful!"

"Is he a good man?"

"I thought he was. But then he did something that showed me he isn't." And was that an understatement, or what? Took the money, then ran hard and fast the other way.

"Well, I'm sorry to hear that." She patted Aubrey's knee again. "But you'll have to tell him soon, and, after you talk, you both can figure out how you want to handle this."

The thought of telling Enzo made her feel faint all over again. He'd be horrified to be having a child at all, let alone with her, since he obviously didn't feel any of the things for her that she'd believed he did. Not to mention he'd all but accused her of trying to trap him when she came to work at the clinic. He'd probably think this was proof of that, since she must have gotten pregnant that very first time they were together. "I don't think I'll tell him, Maggie. I'll just raise it myself. He lives halfway across the world, anyway."

"Italy isn't exactly halfway across the world from the east coast of the US, now, is it?" Maggie said with a chiding smile. "And do you really want to raise a child alone? Have it grow up like you did, always wondering who your dad was?"

Everything inside her stilled at Maggie's words. All the memories came tumbling back, all the fantasies, all the melancholy she'd felt her whole life knowing that her father must not love her, because if he did he'd come around sometimes. Memories of drawing pictures, imagining who he might be. A pilot or a football player or a dragon slayer. Memories of asking her mother questions that were never answered. Memories of that sad, empty feeling inside that other kids had a dad, knew who he was, and spent happy times with him.

They never had to imagine who he might be, because they knew.

She lifted her gaze to Maggie's face and reached for her gnarled hand. "Thank you. You're right. No matter how hard it will be to tell him, I have to. I can't let my baby grow up like I did, not knowing. Because that was the only thing about my life that wasn't good."

"That's my girl." Maggie's hand squeezed hers. "And do it soon, or otherwise you'll be stewing about it instead of planning your future, and the future of your baby."

"Thanks so much for your good advice." She leaned forward to hug the woman who'd always been there for her since she was eight years old. "I feel so lucky to have had both you and Mom in my life. Two people who loved me and who I knew always had my back."

It was true. And as she pictured Enzo's impish smile, remembering how wonderful he'd been with little Benedetto, reassuring him and fixing his bike, and with all the other children they'd taken care of, she knew, in her heart, that he'd be there for his own child. Not what he'd planned maybe, but he would be. Yes, he'd used her in a way that hurt even more than her father's betrayal. One thing she knew for sure, though?

Family was important to him.

"You know, I think I'm going to call him right now, before I lose my nerve. Get it over with."

"Way to go," Maggie said, and the high-five

hand-slap the older woman gave her, as she'd done since Aubrey was a kid, actually managed to make her smile as she faced the toughest thing she'd ever done.

"I don't understand why you can't give me her address," he said to yet another UWWHA employee. "She worked for me!"

Enzo felt as if all he'd done since he'd gotten back to Venice was pace the floor somewhere. His other house, the clinic, the walkway streaming with people as he'd spoken with his lawyer and the UWWHA and the guy he'd bought his house back from, since he'd been renting it to Aubrey before she'd had to move out.

Pacing this house, too. The one he now owned only because of Aubrey. He'd made so many of the calls from here, now that he'd moved back, because this house somehow felt as if Aubrey were a part of it. But every person he'd reached had claimed they either didn't have her address, or couldn't legally give it to him.

He was close to pointing out he was Italian royalty to see if that loosened their tight lips, which was something he never did. But if he had to, he would, and just as he opened his mouth to see if that would work he heard another call coming in. When he looked at his phone to see who it was, he almost fell over.

"I have to take this call." He abruptly hung up on the person and punched the answer button with a shaking hand. "Aubrey."

"Hi, Enzo." The sound of her voice poured into him like the finest wine, and his fingers tightened on the phone, holding it like a lifeline. "I… I have to talk to you about something. Something important."

"I have to talk to you about something important, too." *Dio*, his heart felt as if it were pounding in his throat, making it hard to breathe. "I've been trying to get your address to send you a letter about it. You need to know that the money transfer from your trust wasn't supposed to go through. It was supposed to go back to you because I couldn't accept it, but there was a mistake and it went through anyway."

The silence from the other end rang in his ears. It struck him that he hadn't thanked her for her incredible generosity, even though he couldn't take the money, and stumbled to get it out coherently. "And I want to thank you for…for caring about the house and I do own it now, so thank you, it's amazing to have it when I thought there was no way it could happen, but I'm in the process of raising the money to pay you back. With interest. So you don't need to worry about that."

He cursed under his breath, knowing he sounded like a raging idiot. But he might never have the chance to talk to her again, and the stress of that knowledge made it difficult to know, exactly, what to say. Difficult to remember how to talk at all.

More silence. "Hello? Are you there?"

"You were going to send me a letter."

She said it in a flat voice as a statement, not a question, and Enzo hurried to answer. "Yes, I wanted to tell you all that I just said, about the mistake, and that I was going to make it right."

"Make it right." Another flat statement. "Picking up the phone was out of the question because you didn't want to talk to me, apparently."

It was true, he hadn't wanted to talk to her. Hadn't wanted to risk letting her know how much he'd come to care for her, had needed to keep her safe and far away from a man who couldn't be the kind of lover she deserved. "It wasn't that I didn't want to talk to you, it was—"

"Save it. I don't need any explanation. It was all crystal clear. You got the money, then suddenly we were working different shifts, you weren't answering *my* phone calls, then you disappear to Tuscany without a word to me. I may not be very smart, but I figured out pretty fast that our...relationship wasn't as it had seemed to me."

"Aubrey." Horror left him frozen to the floor. Did she really think he was that kind of monster? Hearing her voice so hard and cold showed that the awful truth was that she did. "That's not how it happened. I enjoyed our time together. I—"

"Again, save it, please. That's not what I called about. I'm calling about the time we enjoyed together, unfortunately."

Surely, after lambasting him for the past few minutes, she wasn't about to tell him she wanted to see him again, was she? And if she did, what should he say? He'd already told her he was a bad bet, which she apparently fully believed.

This time, he was the one who stayed silent, deciding he'd blabbered and upset her too much already and needed to listen instead.

"I hope you're sitting down, because—" he heard her draw a deep breath "—I'm pregnant. And you're the father."

"What?" The floor beneath his feet felt as if it were moving, and he had to try twice before he could say more. "How do you know?"

"How do I know that I'm pregnant, or that you're the father? Thanks for the insult."

That hard voice had gotten even harder, which kept him from saying, *both*. He stumbled to a chair to sit and try to process the grenade that she'd dropped in his lap.

Thoughts of his brother slowly came to mind, about Shay showing up pregnant and his wondering if that had been her plan all along. Wondering about Aubrey, too, and now he couldn't help but wonder again how much Shay had told her about the Affini family trust that said his properties would all come to him if he married and produced an heir by age thirty-five.

"I know this is a shock. It was for me, too."

Her voice had softened into the Aubrey he knew. He absorbed the sound of it, and as he did his blood seemed to finally start pumping again, reducing the numbness he'd felt creep through every muscle at her stunning announcement.

He thought of all the wonderful things he knew about her. The way she stepped up to take care of everyone around her. Her bravery facing her fear of the water. Her adventurous spirit, and her sweetness with patients and with him. Her genuine love for the architecture and history of the city he loved, too.

The truth came as clear as the glass windows in his library that she'd admired.

She hadn't done this on purpose. She hadn't planned to manipulate him or force him into marriage. She hadn't wanted anything from him, other than the very special time they'd spent together. Instead, she'd given him so much, expecting nothing but his friendship and caring in return.

"We need to talk." He wasn't sure about what, other than their baby. Confusion and fear blurred his vision, and he needed time to think. But he had to see her. Look into her eyes and see her beautiful face as they worked through how to handle this. "Come back to Venice. Or I'll come see you. Which would you rather?"

"Neither. There's no reason for us to see one another right now. I knew I had a responsibility to you and to our baby to tell you, and I've done that." He heard the sudden tears in her voice, heard her breathe in a long, shuddery breath, and the sound of her distress made him want to reach through the phone and hold her close. Let her know that he was here for her. Tell her it would somehow be okay.

"I should be available to you if—"

"There's no 'should' in this. I don't want you to do anything you don't want to do. I'm not like your mother, Enzo, who kept a man in her life who didn't love her. I'm perfectly fine on my own. I'll let you know when it's getting near the time it will be born. We can talk then about when you can come see it, and how we're going to handle things after that."

"Aubrey, no. We need to—"

"*Arrivederci*, Enzo."

The way she said goodbye, low and gentle, pulled hard at his heart. Because goodbye sounded so final, and he realized he'd avoided saying that to her before by leaving Venice altogether. Her soft tone reminded him of the times they'd made love, and that she'd spoken to him that way after being so angry, and then telling him she didn't want to see him, brought a lump to his throat, too.

He sat with the silent phone held limply in his hand for a long time after she'd hung up, finally getting up to move in a slow stride that was far different than the agitated pacing he'd been doing before she called.

Dio mio. A baby. A child created through lovemaking as he'd never experienced in his life, with a woman so beautiful and special in every possible way. Missing her filled him with a hollow ache. Of not getting to see her joyous smile, or feel her silky skin, or tease her inquisitive mind. Of never again sharing coffee with her, or holding her close on a boat ride, or listening to her many knowledgeable ideas.

He moved through his mother's house—his house—and thought of Aubrey as he had nearly every moment since he'd been back. Had slept in a different bedroom than the one she'd used because he couldn't bear to be in it without seeing her beautiful hair spilling across the pillow, her eyes smiling at him as she awakened, feeling her warm, soft body tucked closely against his.

Thought about her as he wandered through each room, picking up the artwork and little things she'd admired. Touched the books in the library she'd loved, and thought about her comments about the windows, and the light in the room. Looked up at the painting on the ceiling, and realized one of the angels depicted there looked a little like her.

Slowly, he made his way into the office he'd just recently brought all his things to, and picked up the deed to the house. Stared at it for a long time, and as he did the confusion he felt lifted, cleared, and he knew with absolute certainty what he wanted to do. Because there was nothing confusing about how he felt about Aubrey.

He loved her.

Loved her in a way he'd never loved anyone before. A woman who deserved a man who would care for her and be loyal and faithful to her forever. He wanted to be that man, so much that for a long moment he tried to convince himself he could be. But he was his father's son, and he couldn't bear to ever hurt her the way his father had hurt his mother.

He couldn't give himself to her, because that wouldn't be the kind of gift she deserved. There was one thing, though, that he could give her. The perfect and right thing. He would give this house to the woman he loved, and to the unborn child they'd made together. She loved Venice, had said she loved this house, and he knew she would bring their child here to learn its history, and discover his or her own deep heritage. An Affini growing up right here where he and Dante had grown up. A new child following a long line of generations of his mother's family, and he actually smiled when he pictured his mother smiling, too, because he knew she would be.

Of course he'd be a part of his baby's life and help it grow up as best he could. Seeing Aubrey and not being able to hold her and love her would unbearably hurt, he knew, but he'd keep away from her as much as possible to protect them both.

CHAPTER FOURTEEN

AUBREY STILLED WHEN she saw the certified letter postmarked from Venice, Italy. There were two possibilities what it could be. One: that it was from the UWWHA about the brief time she'd worked there. Or two: it was from Enzo.

With her heart skipping around and her stomach tight, she opened the envelope and slid out a folded letter, along with an official-looking document and a piece of stiff manila paper. Then stared at the document, her heart now in her throat, barely able to process what she was looking at.

The deed to Enzo's house. With her name on it. What in the world…?

With shaking hands, she slowly unfolded the letter, handwritten in the familiar bold scrawl she'd seen Enzo use on clinic paperwork and prescriptions.

Dear Aubrey,

It is my privilege to be able to give you and our baby this house beloved by my mother's family, by her, and by me. I believe it was beloved by you, too, in the short time you were here.

Thinking of our child spending time there with his or her very special mother makes me smile more than anything has made me smile in a long time. Except for my time with you, because that brought me many smiles, as well.

I hope you'll decide to live there at least part of the year, which also will give me a chance to spend time with our child while you're in Venice. Also know, of course, that if you choose to stay in the States, I'll visit regularly to be a part of our baby's life.

I look forward to hearing from you when the time comes for our bimba *to be born, be-*

cause I want so much to be there with you for
what will be an incredible moment in both of
our lives.
All my love,
Enzo

Aubrey stared at the letter, then the deed, then
read the letter three more times, not quite believing what she was seeing.

He'd given her the house he grew up in? The
house he loved so much; that he'd worked so hard
to try to buy back? The house that had been so
important to him, he'd made her think he liked
her so she'd help with the purchase?

Except, that obviously couldn't be true. If it
was, she wouldn't be holding this deed in her
hand.

She laid the deed and letter on the kitchen
counter and picked up the third paper that had
been enclosed with them in the envelope, turning
it over to see what it was. Then what little breath
she had left swooshed from her lungs.

It was the watercolor painting of Enzo's home
they'd seen when they walked along the waterside.

The place considered to be a particularly special example of an amazing house in a city full of incredible houses. The rich colors leaped from the page, bringing memories of the short time she'd been able to live there, of making love there with Enzo, of his plans to restore it to its original glory.

It is my privilege to be able to give you and our baby this house beloved by my mother's family, by her, and by me.

She stared at those words on Enzo's letter, then looked back at the beautiful painting he'd obviously made a special effort to get for her.

Did her being wrong about him using her to buy the house for himself mean she could also be wrong about how Enzo felt about her? Was there any way it was possible that he loved her the way she loved him?

All my love,
Enzo

Slowly, she shook her head. Who knew, maybe a deceitfully charming man like him signed letters like that all the time. But as she thought about him, this crazy man she stupidly still loved, the man who'd given her this incredible gift and, unexpectedly, a baby as well, she knew that, no matter how hard it might be, she had to find out.

The thought of baring her soul and telling him how much she loved him felt beyond terrifying. But hadn't he said she was brave? Amazing to face her fears?

Dealing with her fear of water was a good thing, but not essential to happiness and living her life to the fullest. Risking telling Enzo she loved him? Shoving that fear aside to find out if maybe he loved her, too? That was worth everything. She had nothing to lose but her pride, right? And if he didn't, she'd simply be standing in the same place she stood right now.

A place that didn't feel nearly full enough without Enzo by her side.

How the tiny premature infants in the neonatal intensive care unit at the Hospital San Pietro could stand the glare of harsh white light above them was beyond Enzo. Not to mention the annoyance of the steadily beeping screens above the bassinets, and the way they were hooked up to IVs and external monitors of all kinds. He'd never been bothered by it before, when he'd taken care of patients in the hospital, and knowing all that was helping them get well. But thankfully the babies seemed utterly oblivious to it, sleeping peacefully.

Especially his new little niece, Sophia Maria Affini.

Looking at her tiny face, he couldn't help but think about how much his mother, with only two mischievous sons growing up in her house, would have loved having a granddaughter. Hoped that maybe his niece might look a little like her someday. Dante was convinced that the baby looked just like him, except for the heart shape of her face like Shay's.

Enzo personally thought that, at the moment, the skinny baby looked more like a tiny monkey than his mother or brother or sister-in-law, but he'd kept that to himself. Had a feeling Dante wouldn't appreciate that opinion.

What would his own child look like? Would it be a girl with gray-blue eyes and golden-brown hair? A boy with his beautiful mother's coloring, or would it, girl or boy, be darkly Italian?

Never had he imagined his brother or himself having a new little life they were responsible for. And yet staring at Sophia Maria's tiny pink face, he knew both he and Dante had been given an amazing gift. Gifts they hadn't planned on, and maybe didn't deserve, but perhaps that was the best kind of gift. The kind you didn't even know you wanted until you held it in your hands.

His gift wasn't here yet, wouldn't be for too many months, and it took nearly all his strength to not hop on a plane, find Aubrey, and bring her back to Venice until their baby was born. Take care of her, and be there for her in any way she wanted him to be.

Except she'd made it very clear she didn't want that. Respecting her wishes was more important than his need to see her. More important than pandering to his own desires, which was something he'd spent his lifetime doing. But that was about to change. Soon he'd have a new life to think about, and he'd already realized that having a child was going to make him a better man.

"Goodbye, little one." He patted the glass surrounding the sleeping infant. "Sweet dreams, and your uncle Enzo will come see you again very soon."

He pushed to his feet and headed to a local restaurant, leaving with his dinner in a bag to head back to his house. The worry that had been nagging at him for the past few days came back as soon as he was in his boat.

Why hadn't Aubrey ever called him about the deed? What if she hadn't gotten it?

Then told himself—again—that his worry about that was stupid. He'd received notice that it had been delivered to her house and signed for, hadn't he? So the reason he hadn't heard from her was obvious.

Clearly, she still didn't want to talk to him, and he could hardly blame her. Hadn't he avoided calling her from the day he'd left for Tuscany while she was still in Venice? He probably wouldn't have talked to her ever again if she weren't pregnant with his baby, and thinking about that reality squeezed his heart so hard he wondered how it could continue beating.

He pulled the boat up to his dock and secured it, leaning down to grab the dinner he'd be eating alone, and a heavy feeling hung on his shoulders. He couldn't remember ever feeling lonely before, but loving Aubrey and missing her were all new things he would just have to get used to.

He fished his house key from his pocket as he rounded the corner to the front door, stopping abruptly when he saw two sandaled feet with pink toenails…shapely legs stretched across his doorstep. He let his gaze travel up those beautiful legs to the yellow skirt skimming her thighs, and his stomach dived and pitched and smashed right into his heart at the sight.

"Aubrey?"

"*Buonasera*, Enzo."

He stared down into the eyes he'd missed so

much, at the curve of her sweet lips, and practically fell to his knees as he crouched down in front of her, dropping the bag to reach for her hands. "Are you all right? Is something wrong?"

"I'm fine. The baby is fine, too."

His heart started up again in slow, lurching thuds as he sucked in a steadying breath. "Then why are you here, sitting on a hard stone step? You need to take better care of yourself! How did you even know I would be here? You might have sat there for hours, getting a chill." He lifted her to her feet and it was all he could do to not pull her into his arms and beg her to stay with him forever.

"I got Shay to ask Dante which house you were living in, and if you were in Venice. Then I talked to Nora, and she told me you'd worked today. Then I came here, though I admit I was a little worried you might not come home, or would have some woman with you."

He could tell the joking tone and half smile on her face were forced, and her gaze was searching his for something, but he had no idea what.

"I haven't wanted to be with another woman since you left Venice that first time." Had wondered if he'd want to be with anyone other than Aubrey ever again. "For heaven's sake, please get up off the hard pavement and tell me why you're here."

He knew why he wanted her to be here, which was to take up where they'd left off, but he couldn't let that happen, could he? His important reason and conviction about staying away from her faded from memory as he absorbed the feel of her hands in his, that she was here in this house again—her house now—where every room he went into she was on his mind and in his heart.

"Why I'm here? Are you accusing me of stalking you again?"

"You're ridiculous," he managed to mutter. "I want you to be here, but I'm confused because you said you didn't want to see me."

"I didn't. But now I'm here because I have something to say that couldn't be said on the phone."

She licked her lips and he could almost see her

shoring up the inner strength she had that made her fight her fear of water and go for what she wanted.

"What?"

"I'm here to tell you that I love you. Not because I'm pregnant with your baby, because I loved you before I left Venice. I think I fell a little in love with you that very first night we were together, and every time I was with you, I fell a little harder. When you fixed Benedetto's bike, and when you were so sweet with the lady who had heart failure. When you held me to make me feel safe on the water, and when you rescued that bird. And I decided that I had to tell you. Even if you don't love me back, I wanted you to know."

His heart pounded hard in his chest as he looked into the beautiful eyes he loved, reflecting that love right back at him. To see it there humbled him more than he'd ever been humbled in his life, because he knew he'd never done a thing to deserve the love of a woman like her.

She took a step forward, looking up at him with hope and fear and uncertainty swimming in the blue-gray depths of her eyes. His hands closed around her arms, but he didn't let himself pull her close. Didn't speak. Didn't know what to say or how to say it.

"Enzo, I flew across the ocean to tell you I love you, and to see if you might love me, too. I need for you to give me an honest answer back. Please. That's all I'm asking for."

All she was asking for. So easy to give her the honest answer she wanted, but so incredibly hard to know if he should. "You know I'm a bad bet, Aubrey. Remember?"

"I don't believe that. You might not love me back, but, no matter what, I would bet on you any day." She brought one of her hands to his cheek. "You're a good man. A special man. A man who would give the house he loves to a woman he may not love, and to an unborn child he didn't plan on and hasn't even met yet. That tells me you have the kind of deep moral character that should tell *you* that you're not at all like your father."

Admiration had joined the other emotions in the eyes gazing into his, and his hands tightened to tug her closer. Whether or not she was right, he owed her the truth. "I do love you, Aubrey. I love you more than I knew it was possible to love a woman. And because I love you so much, I'm afraid to ask you to be with me forever. I'm afraid I might hurt you, and I couldn't bear for that to happen."

"You helped me with my fear of the water. What do you say I help you with your fear of hurting me? We spend the next six months making love and fixing up this house and working and adventuring together. After little Prince or Princess Affini shows up, if you feel like being with another woman, feel those bad genes taking over, I won't try to keep you. You can decide then to let me go. What do you say?"

Another emotion in those eyes. Trust. So clear and real, it brought a thick lump to his throat. Listening to her words, looking into her eyes as he held her close, made him finally know.

He'd never be like his father.

Aubrey was the only woman he would always want to be with. To love her and cherish her and do whatever he could for her. He wanted to marry her and spend the rest of his life with her and be the best bet she'd ever made in her life.

"What do I say?" His answer was to kiss her. Softly and slowly the way he'd thought about kissing her every hour of every day for the past six weeks, breathing in her sweet scent, tasting the lips he'd never thought he'd get to taste again.

When she eventually broke the kiss and leaned back, she gave him the smile that had dazzled him from that very first day they'd met. He held both their hands to the slightly rounded belly that, incredibly, held the baby they'd created together, and pressed his forehead to hers, swallowing down the emotion overwhelming him. "I say that I don't need six months. I only need as much time as you want to put a wedding together. Can't have little one born out of wedlock, can we?"

"I guess Prince or Princess Affini won't need that kind of attention from the tabloids." She wrapped her arms around his neck. "What do you think about getting married on a boat out on the lagoon?"

He laughed against her mouth. "A celebration of both of us moving past our fears? I can't think of anything better than that."

EPILOGUE

AUBREY KNEW THAT no one expected peace and quiet at a one-year-old's birthday party, but she had to wonder if the insistent banging on the ancient *terrazzo* floor just might be getting on the nerves of at least one of the thirty or so guests by now.

She crouched down next to her baby son, Gabriel Dante Affini, and waved a new toy in front of him. His instantly fascinated eyes were so like his daddy's, it filled her heart with overwhelming emotion the way it did every time she looked at him. Gabriel's focus switched to the dangling, colorful rings from the plastic hammer he had been pounding.

"How are we ever going to get the renovation on this house finished if you won't let him work on it?" Enzo said in her ear as he leaned over both of them, his warm lips sliding down her cheek while his big hand rested on their son's soft black hair.

"With or without his help, we have a long way to go, and I think he's examined the floor enough for today. But we'll get there, don't you worry." She lifted her lips to meet his, still amazed that this man was hers. That he loved her as much as she loved him. That the touch of his mouth always made her feel breathless. "Even though it's not close to livable yet, I'm so happy we decided to have Sophia Maria's one-year birthday party here. In the house where her *nonna* and daddy and uncle grew up. Do you think the smell of paint and sawdust will make everyone extra hungry for the cake?"

Enzo chuckled and glanced over at his niece, who seemed deeply focused on taking off her pink birthday hat, then trying to put it back on again, much to her parents' amusement. "I find the construction scent very pleasing and appetizing. But not nearly as pleasing and appetizing as you."

His mouth met hers again for a long kiss that

had her clutching his shirt as he sat on the floor to pull her close, until something fluttered into their faces to separate them.

Aubrey and Enzo both turned to see the birthday hat lying between them, and Sophia laughing as she lurched in her adorable, learning-to-walk way to retrieve it.

"Hey, you two, enough of that. This is a birthday party, not a date night," Dante jokingly chided as he pulled Shay close against him.

"Every night is date night with my wife," Enzo responded with a grin. "And the sooner your daughter opens her presents, the sooner we can get on with our date."

"Enzo!" Aubrey swatted his arm as Dante and Shay laughed.

"My brother and I have always had an understanding. And today that means he knows I'd just as soon finish celebrating, too, then get home with my wife and daughter to celebrate some more. After Sophia Maria is in bed." Dante kissed Shay's forehead as she rested against his shoulder, turning to Aubrey with a wide smile.

"We had no idea what we were getting ourselves into when we came to Italy, did we?"

"No, we sure didn't." Aubrey watched her handsome husband lift their baby into his arms, who gently bonked him on the head with the plastic hammer as Gabriel laughed. "I thought I was coming here to work. To cure my fear of water and have an adventure. And what did I get?"

She stood to lean over Enzo and Gabriel, wrapping her arms around them. Holding them close to the wonder that filled her heart.

"I don't know, *bellezza*," Enzo murmured against her temple. "What did you get?"

The answer was so enormous, a mere sentence couldn't cover it. "I got our beautiful son. A new life and new dreams. This wonderful and special house. And you." She kissed him again, not caring if Dante complained. "My perfect and amazing husband, who I'm betting will keep making me happy every day for the rest of my life."

* * * * *

If you missed the first story in the
ROYAL SPRING BABIES *duet, check out*

HIS PREGNANT ROYAL BRIDE
by Amy Ruttan

*And if you enjoyed this story, check out these
other great reads from Robin Gianna*

*REUNITED WITH HIS RUNAWAY BRIDE
THE PRINCE AND THE MIDWIFE
HER CHRISTMAS BABY BUMP
HER GREEK DOCTOR'S PROPOSAL*

All available now!

MILLS & BOON®
Large Print Medical

October

Their One Night Baby	Carol Marinelli
Forbidden to the Playboy Surgeon	Fiona Lowe
A Mother to Make a Family	Emily Forbes
The Nurse's Baby Secret	Janice Lynn
The Boss Who Stole Her Heart	Jennifer Taylor
Reunited by Their Pregnancy Surprise	Louisa Heaton

November

Mummy, Nurse...Duchess?	Kate Hardy
Falling for the Foster Mum	Karin Baine
The Doctor and the Princess	Scarlet Wilson
Miracle for the Neurosurgeon	Lynne Marshall
English Rose for the Sicilian Doc	Annie Claydon
Engaged to the Doctor Sheikh	Meredith Webber

December

Healing the Sheikh's Heart	Annie O'Neil
A Life-Saving Reunion	Alison Roberts
The Surgeon's Cinderella	Susan Carlisle
Saved by Doctor Dreamy	Dianne Drake
Pregnant with the Boss's Baby	Sue MacKay
Reunited with His Runaway Doc	Lucy Clark

MILLS & BOON®
Large Print Medical

January

The Surrogate's Unexpected Miracle	Alison Roberts
Convenient Marriage, Surprise Twins	Amy Ruttan
The Doctor's Secret Son	Janice Lynn
Reforming the Playboy	Karin Baine
Their Double Baby Gift	Louisa Heaton
Saving Baby Amy	Annie Claydon

February

Tempted by the Bridesmaid	Annie O'Neil
Claiming His Pregnant Princess	Annie O'Neil
A Miracle for the Baby Doctor	Meredith Webber
Stolen Kisses with Her Boss	Susan Carlisle
Encounter with a Commanding Officer	Charlotte Hawkes
Rebel Doc on Her Doorstep	Lucy Ryder

March

The Doctor's Forbidden Temptation	Tina Beckett
From Passion to Pregnancy	Tina Beckett
The Midwife's Longed-For Baby	Caroline Anderson
One Night That Changed Her Life	Emily Forbes
The Prince's Cinderella Bride	Amalie Berlin
Bride for the Single Dad	Jennifer Taylor

MILLS & BOON®
Large Print – September 2017

ROMANCE

The Sheikh's Bought Wife	Sharon Kendrick
The Innocent's Shameful Secret	Sara Craven
The Magnate's Tempestuous Marriage	Miranda Lee
The Forced Bride of Alazar	Kate Hewitt
Bound by the Sultan's Baby	Carol Marinelli
Blackmailed Down the Aisle	Louise Fuller
Di Marcello's Secret Son	Rachael Thomas
Conveniently Wed to the Greek	Kandy Shepherd
His Shy Cinderella	Kate Hardy
Falling for the Rebel Princess	Ellie Darkins
Claimed by the Wealthy Magnate	Nina Milne

HISTORICAL

The Secret Marriage Pact	Georgie Lee
A Warriner to Protect Her	Virginia Heath
Claiming His Defiant Miss	Bronwyn Scott
Rumours at Court (Rumors at Court)	Blythe Gifford
The Duke's Unexpected Bride	Lara Temple

MEDICAL

Their Secret Royal Baby	Carol Marinelli
Her Hot Highland Doc	Annie O'Neil
His Pregnant Royal Bride	Amy Ruttan
Baby Surprise for the Doctor Prince	Robin Gianna
Resisting Her Army Doc Rival	Sue MacKay
A Month to Marry the Midwife	Fiona McArthur

0817 GEN STD LP

MILLS & BOON®

Why shop at millsandboon.co.uk?

Each year, thousands of romance readers find their perfect read at millsandboon.co.uk. That's because we're passionate about bringing you the very best romantic fiction. Here are some of the advantages of shopping at www.millsandboon.co.uk:

* **Get new books first**—you'll be able to buy your favourite books one month before they hit the shops

* **Get exclusive discounts**—you'll also be able to buy our specially created monthly collections, with up to 50% off the RRP

* **Find your favourite authors**—latest news, interviews and new releases for all your favourite authors and series on our website, plus ideas for what to try next

* **Join in**—once you've bought your favourite books, don't forget to register with us to rate, review and join in the discussions

Visit **www.millsandboon.co.uk**
for all this and more today!